Little Journeys Into Storyland

LITTLE JOURNEYS
Into Storyland

◆◆◆◆◆◆

Stories That Will Live and Lift

◆◆◆◆◆◆

By

Louis B. Reynolds

and

Charles L. Paddock

SOUTHERN PUBLISHING ASSOCIATION
Nashville, Tennessee
(Printed in U. S. A.)

Between the dark and the daylight, when the night is beginning to lower,
Comes a pause in the day's occupations, that is known as the Children's Hour.
—Henry W. Longfellow.

George Washington Carver studied the secrets of humble plants.

A Boy Traded for a Horse

THERE alighted from a train in Washington one morning, an elderly gentleman. His form was stooped; his face, kind and gentle. He wore a simple cloth cap on his head, carried a home-made box under his arm, and seemed a bit bewildered by the hurrying crowds of people. Porters were rushing up and down the station platform, peering into this car and that, and seemed to be looking for someone. The little old man managed to stop one of them long enough to ask some questions, but the redcap didn't have time.

"Sorry, pop," he said, "I don't have time to give you any directions now. We're trying to find a big scientist that's coming in on this train from away down in Alabama."

The bent old man was the great scientist, George Washington Carver, and the porter has perhaps often regretted that he didn't have time that morning to help him. Dr. Carver was on his way to the House of Representatives. The United States Government had invited him there to tell of his work of research and experiment with the peanut.

There were a number of other men appearing at that same time, and each speaker was to have five minutes. As Dr. Carver proceeded to open up his box containing his exhibits before the men of the House of Representatives, some one rudely shouted, "Hurry up, old man!"

But he did not stop his speech in five minutes. The congressmen were deeply interested. For forty-five minutes he talked softly, reverently, of the wonders

11

which God had stored in this common, humble plant.

The world had paid little heed when a baby boy was born in Civil War days in the slave quarters of Moses Carver, on a Missouri plantation, but when he died, many years later, the whole world did him honor, because of the wonderful things he had done for all the world.

George Washington Carver didn't have any birthday celebrations, for he wasn't sure just when he was born, although he thought it must have been in the year 1864. He didn't know who his father was, and he didn't remember his mother. When he was just a baby, slave raiders took him and his mother from their master's home at Diamond Grove, Missouri, into Arkansas. A rescue party went in search of them, but when they caught up with the raiders, the mother had been sold, and they could not locate her. They did some bargaining with the raiding party, and traded a race horse, valued at about $300, for the baby.

The child grew up frail and sickly, and so Moses Carver let him do light work about the house, such as sewing, cooking, washing clothes, etc. I suppose that as a boy he didn't exactly like to do this kind of work; but when he got older he was glad that he had learned to work, for he had to make a living for himself.

From childhood he had loved nature and had a yearning for knowledge. When his tasks in the house were done, he often wandered into the woods and fields, learning what he could about the birds, the trees, flowers, and other plants. At home there was only one book which he could use. It was a blue-backed speller, and he practically memorized it. The Carvers couldn't send him to school, but he determined to go even if it meant hardship for him. Fortunately there was a school near by, to which he could go. He worked at any task he could find, and slept in barns or haylofts until he had finished the course in the simple, one-room school.

When he wanted to go to high school, the lessons he had learned in the Carver home proved useful. He paid a great deal of his expenses by laundering clothes for people in the neighborhood.

When he finished high school, he wrote to the Iowa University and made arrangements to enter there; but when he arrived at the school, he was refused entrance because he was a Negro. He was not discouraged, but immediately started a small laundry, where he worked early and late. Thus he earned and saved his money until he had enough to enter Simpson College at Indianola, Iowa. Here he spent three years, and then four years at Iowa State Agricultural College, paying all his way by house cleaning, scrubbing floors, and washing clothes.

His industry and his genius with plants and soils won the admiration of the board of the school, and he was given a place on the faculty. At that time Booker T. Washington was looking for a man of ability and vision to come to Tuskegee Institute to help better the condition of the Southern Negro. Feeling he could be of service to his people, George Washington Carver readily responded to the call.

Arriving at Tuskegee, he found little equipment with which to work. Many men would have been disgusted and discouraged, but not Carver. He believed in the "start where you are, and use what you have" formula, declaring that it would bring success anywhere.

"The Bible," he often said, "is as important to me as

the laboratory." One of his favorite texts was, "I can do all things through Christ which strengtheneth me." Philippians 4:13. Another was: "In all thy ways acknowledge Him, and He shall direct thy paths." Proverbs 3:6.

With love for his fellow men, and trust in God, he began to "make bricks without straw" at Tuskegee. He lived simply, but sincerely.

He found there a sixteen-acre, sandy, unfertile farm. They had no laboratory. Much of his equipment he made. An empty ink bottle and a wick made an alcohol lamp. A heavy kitchen cup became a mortar, and a flat piece of iron a pulverizer. Beakers were made from bottles found in the school garbage dump. His skillful hands fashioned equipment from scraps of rubber, wire and metal; and soon he had a simple laboratory to begin his experiments.

People told him that he couldn't grow anything on that sandy soil. But it was the only soil he had, and, following a life motto, he started with that. The students were set to work with baskets and buckets, carrying muck and leaf mould from the woods to enrich the sandy, impoverished soil. Soon he was growing two crops of sweet potatoes a year and raising a bale of cotton to an acre, where poor Alabama farmers had been barely existing on their barren farms. Before he arrived, this land had shown a loss of sixteen dollars an acre each year, but under his scientific care it showed a gain.

When he began his work at Tuskegee, there were few vegetable gardens in the district, and the farmers had no chickens, cows, or bees. Because of an unbalanced diet, pellagra was everywhere. But he changed that situation. Today practically every family for miles around has its vegetable garden, cows, and chickens. With a balanced diet, pellagra disappeared. Cotton had been the one crop of the South. Dr. Carver urged the farmers to plant sweet potatoes and peanuts, and then set himself to the task of finding a market for them. From the peanuts he made more than 300 useful articles, among them oils, flour, candy, milk, face powder, floor covering, soap, vinegar, molasses, etc. From the clay soil he made paving brick, pottery, inks, and many other useful articles. He wove beautiful mats from the swamp cattails, and table scarfs from empty feed bags, coloring them with the bright clay dyes. He used stalks of cane and corn for insulating material. From sunflower stalks and the wild hibiscus he manufactured paper. He just couldn't stand to see anything go to waste.

Any information he gathered, he passed on to the farmers free. Not once did he sell a patent or charge for help or information. His ambition was to give rather than to get. When urged to charge for his services, he once said, "God didn't charge for His work in making peanuts grow, and I won't charge for mine."

In a horse and buggy he carried exhibits to the farmers. He printed pamphlets and distributed them widely. He became an expert dietitian and cook, and passed on his recipes to the farmers' wives. One pamphlet was entitled, "One Hundred and Five Different Ways to Prepare the Peanut for the Table." There were recipes for soup, roast, cheese, patties, pie crust, and many other things.

He published a bulletin, "Nature's Garden for Victory and Peace," and in the introduction he quoted that

well-known text from the Bible, "Behold, I have given
you every herb; ... to you it shall be for meat." Genesis
1:29. In it he listed many grasses, weeds, and wild
flowers which, he declared, were good for food.

Naturally, his fame spread abroad, and thousands
went to Tuskegee to see him. Imagine their surprise
when they found him wearing an old weather-beaten cap
and a well worn, frayed, gray sweater.

Thomas Edison tried to get him to come to work with
him, but the offer of $50,000 a year was no temptation.
He preferred to stay in his simple bachelor quarters in
the dormitory at Tuskegee. Medals and awards came
to him for his outstanding service to mankind. Greatness was literally forced upon him, but he remained
humble, gentle, and a sincere Christian, giving God the
glory for all that he had been able to accomplish.

When asked one time how he was able to do so much,
he said, "I have made it a rule to get up every morning
at four. I go into the woods, and there I gather speci-
mens, and study the great lessons that nature is eager to
teach us. Alone in the woods each morning I best hear
and understand God's plans for me."

He was only following in the footsteps of the Master,
of whom it is said, "He rose long before day and spent
much time alone with nature and God."

"The beauty of his life," said a noted educator, "is
that he does not desire publicity, but carries on in a
modest fashion, giving God all the glory for what he has
accomplished. It is refreshing in these days to find a
man so thoroughly scientific, and at the same time so
spiritual."

Few men started life more humbly than did George
Washington Carver; few died more honored; few crowd-

ed more into a life's span than he did. When the radio flashed to the world the news of his death, millions felt that a friend and benefactor had gone. He left the world a better place, and his influence shall ever live.

To honor her singing, Temple University in Philadelphia, Pennsylvania, gave Marian Anderson a Doctor of Music Degree.

How Marian Got Her Violin

N EAR the kitchen door on the back porch, four-year-old Marian sat quietly strumming on a bench. It was her make-believe piano. In this manner she played the spirituals and hymns she had learned at home or at church:

"I got a robe, you got a robe,
All God's children got a robe,
When I get to heaven, going to put on my robe,
Going to shout all over God's heaven."

How she did long for a real piano—an instrument all her own, that would add gaiety and color to the songs of the entire household.

You see, Marian was the oldest of three sisters in the Anderson family. When they were little more than babies, their father had died, and they could not get many of the things that parents usually buy for their little girls. Their mother worked hard to provide the girls with necessary food, and with dresses to wear. An Aunt Mary had come to live with them in order to help. But both Aunt Mary and their mother had to work most of the time outside the home in order to secure money to keep the household going.

Marian helped with the home chores from the time she could first walk. She washed dishes, ran errands, swept the house, and did whatever a little girl could to assist with the work.

When she was six, she began to yearn for a violin. Somewhere she had seen this instrument, and had heard a violinist play. The music had charmed her fancy.

Now she must have an instrument of her own.

But violins are not bought as easily as that. Usually they cost a great deal of money, and poor people, in order to have a violin at all, sacrifice many other things for the privilege. Sometimes they have to pay a long time in small sums. Sometimes the purchaser is required to pay full cash, especially in the case of a used instrument.

From day to day Marian looked to find a violin. In music shops, in antique shops, in pawn shops, and in every likely place she searched. Some were new and therefore very expensive; some were very old; some were without strings or without a bow.

Finally Marian saw one that was just right, and priced near a figure that she might be able to reach within a reasonable time. It was in a pawnshop window, and on it was a little card marked with the price—$3.40.

At once she began to lay by little sums in order to get it. She earned nickels and dimes in any way she could. There were errands to run, chores to do for the neighbors, and there were always steps to be scrubbed. "Scrubbing steps," she explained, "is not nearly so hard as it looks. You just take two pails full of water, and use one for scrubbing with plenty of soap and a stiff brush, and the other for rinsing with clean water and a long-handled mop. If you're working with another little girl, scrubbing is fun. It's about the easiest money I've ever earned."

When it was known that Marian was working to get a violin, friends and the family helped. Her nickels and dimes and pennies increased more rapidly.

All the while she was looking almost daily to see that her prize was not purchased by another. She had even gone inside to test the instrument for herself. She bargained with the man in the pawnshop until he consented to sell it to her for exactly three dollars!

One bright, spring morning she stepped into the shop with the required amount in coins to make the purchase. How happy she was! The shopkeeper was also happy to see the little girl secure her prize. She gave the man three dollars, made a few noises on her purchase, and was off to show her mother, her aunt, and her two sisters the wonderful violin.

Marian Anderson has become one of the world's greatest singers. The violin was her start in music. Her determination to get it was much like the enthusiasm with which she has pursued her musical career until her songs are loved and heard the world over.

Abraham Lincoln earned the love and honor of all people because he championed the cause of the poor and needy.

A Very Kind Man

A BIG, tall, giant of a man, with kind but homely face, was one day making his way along the streets when he overtook a little girl, who evidently was in trouble. From her sobbing and crying, he knew something was wrong. Big as he was, he had a kind heart, and stopped to ask what the trouble might be, and if he could be of any help.

It took a little coaxing on the part of the big, tall stranger, but she finally told him that she had planned to go away on the train, and had asked some one to call and get her trunk and take it to the station. It was almost train time, and no one had come for the trunk. And she must catch the train.

The big, tall man told her to dry her tears and show him where the trunk was. He would take it to the station for her. He soon had the trunk on his back, and carried it to the depot in time for her to buy her ticket. She was a happy little girl, and he was a happy man. His life was made up of just such little acts of kindness.

He was one of the best-loved men of all time, Abraham Lincoln. Some one called him the American Greatheart. He was kind to every one—to little children, to the poor, to his soldiers, to the wives and mothers of the soldiers, even to animals.

Some think it is a sign of weakness to be kind, but it is really a mark of greatness. Few men have had more troubles and perplexities than did Lincoln, yet few men are more sympathetic and considerate.

One day he was busy at the White House talking to

a soldier who had brought important tidings from the battle front. There came a tapping at the door. Being very much absorbed in the business of the hour, he paid no attention to the tapping, and it continued. After a time a boy's voice was heard. "It's Tad, father, unfasten the door."

Lincoln hurriedly unfastened the door, and in scampered little Tad in his nightgown, all ready for bed. He took the little fellow over to the table, and, with the tiny hand in his big hand, he began to tap on the table as he explained to Tad, "You forgot your signals, didn't you? When you want to come in, this is the way to telegraph me—three quick raps followed by two slower ones."

Tad soon had the lesson learned, and, with a goodnight kiss, was off to bed. With the horrors of war tearing at his heart, Lincoln was not too busy to be kind to his little boy.

When he was younger, riding the circuit as an attorney, he was one day traveling from town to town on horseback with a number of friends. Their road led through a dense woods. In a clump of trees they heard a commotion among some birds, and noticed that a baby bird had fallen from its nest. They rode on by, but Lincoln stopped his horse and said, "I will be back in a moment." He returned to where the baby bird lay on the ground. Tenderly he picked it up, and put it back in the nest again.

When he rejoined his friends, one of the young lawyers rather made fun of him. Sneeringly he asked, "Why did you bother yourself and delay us with such a trifle as that?"

Lincoln's reply is an index to his heart: "I can only say this—I feel better for it. I would not sleep tonight if I had left that helpless little creature to perish on the ground."

At another time, when riding on his circuit, he saw a pig mired in a mudhole. The poor animal was worn out from struggling. Lincoln got off his horse and helped the pig from the mud, and went on his way happy in the thought of having helped one of God's creatures.

One day he saw in the waiting room at the White House a small, pale, delicate-looking boy in his teens. There were many others waiting, but the president was touched by the looks of the lad. Lincoln said to him, "Come here, my boy, and tell me what you want."

Timidly the boy told his story. "Mr. President," he said, "I have been a drummer boy in a regiment for two years. My colonel got angry with me and turned me off. I was taken sick and have been in a hospital for a long time. My father died in the army. I have no mother, no brothers and sisters, and—no friends—nobody cares for me."

The great Lincoln's eyes filled with tears. He ordered his assistants to care for the boy, and the little drummer boy's heart was lighter, for he had found a real friend. No wonder Lincoln was loved.

At the time of the war between the North and the South a boy was sentenced to be shot because he had fallen asleep at his post. His case was brought to Lincoln, who, after considering it, said, "I could not think of going into eternity with the blood of that poor young man on my skirts. It is not to be wondered at that a boy raised on a farm, probably in the habit of going to bed at dark, should, when required to watch, fall asleep, and I cannot consent to shoot him for such an act."

And he didn't. He pardoned the lad.

One day an old gentleman, bent with years, and his face lined with care, came to Lincoln with a sad story. His son had committed some crime punishable by death. He was his only boy. He begged the president to save him.

"I am sorry I can do nothing for you," said Lincoln, "Listen to this telegram I received from General Butler yesterday. 'President Lincoln, I pray you do not interfere with the courts-martial of the army. You will destroy all discipline among our soldiers.' "

Lincoln watched closely the expression on the father's face, then he said, "Butler or no Butler, here goes."

He hastily wrote a few words on a slip of paper and handed it to the old gentleman. It read, "Job Smith is not to be shot, until further orders from me. Abraham Lincoln."

The father was disappointed, and the disappointment showed in his face and voice. "Why," said the old gentleman with trembling voice, "I thought it was a pardon. You may order him to be shot next week."

"My friend," replied Lincoln, "I see you are not very well acquainted with me. If your son never dies till orders come from me to shoot him, he will live to be a great deal older than Methuselah."

On another occasion a little woman, whose scant raiment and pinched features showed that she was very poor and had to struggle for a living, got in to see the president, after having waited for several days to see him. In his characteristic, friendly way Mr. Lincoln greeted her, "Well, my good woman, what can I do for you?"

She answered, "My only boy is a soldier. His regiment was near enough to my house for him to take a day and run over and see me. He was arrested as a deserter when he re-entered the lines, and condemned to be shot. He is to be executed tomorrow."

Lincoln quickly arose from his chair. He left many senators, congressmen, and generals waiting to see him, and taking the little mother by the hand, hastened with her to the office of the Secretary of War. She did not know where the boy's regiment was stationed, nor where the execution was to take place. Stanton, who had become disgusted with the President's big-heartedness, begged Lincoln to forget the matter and let the rules of the army be enforced. But the president's big heart wouldn't allow him to do it. He couldn't bear to see a boy shot just for running away for a day to see the best friend any boy ever has—his mother.

In very certain tones Lincoln replied, "I will not be balked in this. Send this message to every headquarters, every fort, and every camp in the United States, 'Let no military execution take place until further orders from me. A. Lincoln.' "

Another mother's heart was gladdened; another life was spared. And Lincoln went to bed that night happier for having been a blessing.

And who doesn't go to bed happier and sleep better for having done a kindness, for having helped some struggling brother or sister along life's way?

Even when a boy, Lincoln had a very tender heart. When the family moved from Indiana to Illinois, they owned a small dog. They moved by wagon, of course, for there were no railroads and no trucks then. The dog had to follow along behind the wagon. They missed the little fellow one day, and after some searching found he had been left on the other side of an ice-filled river. There he sat yelping and whining. Lincoln's father decided that he would not drive the oxen and wagon back across the river just for a dog. They would go on without him. But Abraham could not desert his friend. So he pulled off his shoes and stockings, and waded across the cold, icy river. In a little while he returned the same way, cold and shivering, but with his heart warm and light, and with the little dog friend under his arm. Lincoln said in later years that he was well repaid by the dog's barks and kisses.

It is not likely that we shall ever have any regrets for having been kind to either man or beast.

Jim's Examination

JIM WAS taking the engineering course in a large university, and the time for final examination was approaching. He was anxious about it; in fact, he seemed to be much more concerned about the examination than many of his fellow students. He remarked to a friend that he was studying hard that he might be ready when the test came.

"Aren't you wise to the fact, Jim," his friend asked, "that you can buy a copy of the questions for five dollars, —the very questions which will be asked in the examination?"

"You don't mean that!" said Jim.

"Surely I mean it. Most of the students have bought the questions. They don't have to worry now. Just study up the answers to the questions and you will be ready. Would you like to get a set, Jim?"

"How do they get the questions, and from whom?" inquired Jim.

"I can get you a set. It is a secret, and we don't want to let the news out. But the janitor has been taking carbon paper from the waste baskets, holding them up to a lookingglass and getting the examination questions. He is making some easy money, and the students have been getting good grades without studying."

It was a shock to Jim, and he couldn't get the consent of his conscience to do such a thing. It was a temptation to him. But he fought a battle in his heart, and won. Either he would pass the examination honestly or he would fail in the attempt. He would not deceive.

The student who studies does not fear his teacher's tests.

So he told the lady where he roomed that he wanted to have two or three days alone to study for examination, that he was going away and would leave no address. He didn't want to be bothered. He would return the morning of the examination.

Finding a place where he could study unmolested, he spent two days in reviewing the work that would be covered on examination day. It was a real struggle, for he knew many of the young men and women were having a good time while he worked. They knew the questions which would be asked, and had the answers ready. But he was happy in the struggle. He was being fair.

On examination morning he climbed the steps of the university building with a clear conscience and a light heart. He felt prepared. A number of the students, however, cast glances his way, which he knew very well did not come from any love in their hearts for him. And some of them said, "You're a fool, Jim, for being so particular. Why go to so much effort when you can get along without it? Why wear out your brain studying for examination? You are easy, Jim."

At just one minute before the examination was to begin, the door to the room was unlocked, and the teacher entered, papers in hand. He seemed to have an unusually serious look on his face. When all was quiet he said, "Students, we have made a rather startling discovery. The examination papers have been tampered with, and it has been made possible for any one who wished to do so to buy the examination questions for a small sum of money. This news came as a real shock to us. So it became necessary for a number of the faculty to sit up all night last night writing out new questions. But they are ready for you, and you may begin to write."

Faces paled, some reddened, others showed signs of real disappointment. There was tenseness in the air. The examination papers were passed out. Some made an attempt to write, but others got up and walked out. They knew there was no use trying, for they had not studied.

In Jim's heart there was a sense of real joy, a feeling of victory, a happiness that he had been man enough to be honest. He with a number of others wrote their examinations. And Jim passed with honors.

He resolved then and there that he would always be fair and honest.

Wise Old Tom

SOME people think cats are stupid, and I thought so, too, for a long time. I changed my mind, however, after some observations. I always felt that dogs had brains and used them, but somehow or other I couldn't feel that way about a cat. It was because I didn't know cats.

One day our little boy of seven came home with a fluffy little kitten in his arms. We supposed it belonged to a neighbor, and that he had just brought it home to show it to us. But no, he wanted to keep it. I wasn't at all enthusiastic about it, but we had some mice about the place, and his mother finally said he might have the kitten. It was named Tommy, which, when it grew older, was shortened to just plain Tom. Tom became one of the family, and really won his way into our hearts.

One spring it was decided that we would go on a trip, and the question arose as to what we should do with Tom. We felt we wouldn't have any trouble in getting some one to care for him, for he had a lovely disposition, and made friends of those who called to visit us. On learning of our plans, some friends asked if they might take Tom and care for him. So arrangements were made for him to be taken to their home the day we left.

They lived on the other side of a big city, about five miles away from our home. So Tom had to be taken across the city. We put him in a cloth bag, much to his displeasure, put him in the back of the car and took him across town. You may wonder why we had to put him in a sack. We felt it would be just as well if he didn't

Cats stupid? Ask the person who has one, and he will tell you how smart cats are

see where he was going, for we had heard of dogs and cats trying to find their way back home again. Surely old Tom in a bag couldn't see where we went, and he wouldn't attempt to go back home.

When we got to the home of our friends, we picked up bag, cat and all, and took them into the house. Tom was happy to get out of the sack, but didn't feel at all at home. We left him there, thinking he would adjust himself to his new surroundings in a few hours.

The first time they opened the door he darted out and disappeared. Of course, they were worried about him, but they could not find him. A few days later he was seen back at our home. Our neighbors watched him try to get into the house. They wondered if we would go away and leave the cat without food and shelter. He stayed around for several days and then was not seen any more. He went back across town to our friend's home again.

We received a letter from them which said, "Old Tom is back. He was tired and hungry, and is now glad to stay with us." He made himself at home and stayed there contentedly until we returned some weeks later.

It may be hard to believe, but he found his way across that city—five miles back—to our home, stayed there until convinced that we were not there, and then went back across the city again to this friend's home. How did he know his way? I cannot tell you. Not many people could do that without help from someone —how helpless and lost we feel in a strange city! But this poor dumb creature made the trip without any aid from anyone.

Some months ago I was down to Uncle Jack Miner's home just across the river from Detroit. He has a wonderful bird sanctuary there, and is known everywhere as " the man who made the wild goose tame." The morning I was there, some 12,000 wild geese were just rising into the air after having had their breakfast with Uncle Jack. As you know, these geese go north for nesting in the spring, and then in the late fall fly south again. On their journey north in the spring they stop for a week or two with Uncle Jack, and then visit him again in the fall as they return south.

How do they know where Uncle Jack lives? They fly thousands of miles over countless farms, over hundreds of miles of waste land, over lakes and rivers. But they know where Uncle Jack lives, and visit him regularly. How do they know the way to this little farm there on the shores of Lake Erie?

We have a little bird house on a post out in our garden. It is really a neat little home built especially for Jenny Wren. It wasn't on the post long before two busy, chattering little birds were carrying sticks for a nest, and in a few weeks we heard noises inside which told us there must be babies there. Of course, we saw the parents carrying bugs and worms into the house too. The weeks came and went and we were really sorry to see them leave us in the fall. But early next spring they were back again,—the same two birds to the same little house. For several years they have gone away in the fall and returned in the spring.

Where did they go? They flew hundreds of miles south to a warmer climate, then when it was time for spring, they came north again, and somehow found their way right to our little garden spot and to their cozy little home. How did they know it was spring and time to go north again? How did they know north from south? Why didn't they fly west or east instead of north? How did they know where to go when they got started north? We sometimes have trouble in finding our way when we have a road map and are following roads that are all numbered.

Uncle Jack Miner says that when he was a boy, he often found a big, hard-shelled turtle wandering around near a stream. He would pick him up by the tail and carry him through the tall grass some distance from the stream which was his home. The old fellow would stretch his long neck around, seeming to take his bearings, then turn around and start back toward the stream again. How did he know the way back?

I read a very interesting story in a newspaper one morning. It told of a homing pigeon named Old Sleepy. His home was in St. Thomas, Ontario. He was taken by train to Oklahoma City, 1,013 miles away, and released from his cage on the morning of July 24. On July 31, just one week later, this bird reached home, tired, and hungry. When an aviator starts on a flight, he has many delicate instruments to guide him in his course, but Old Sleepy had only the homing instinct which God has placed in his heart.

F. H. Sidney tells an interesting story of a toad that lived in his garden. He had seen Mr. Toad there often and wondered if he were carried away, whether he would find his way back. He put a tag on the toad, and took him through the city of Boston to a spot ten miles from his home. It was just ten minutes to eleven at night when he let the little fellow out of the box. He blinked his eyes a few times and started toward home. The next evening at 6:15, when watering his garden, Mr. Sidney found the dusty little toad, with the tag at-

tached to his hind leg. He had hopped the ten miles
back home in less than twenty hours.

John Burroughs once bought a drake from a farmer
living two miles away. The duck was delivered to him
in a bag. It was shut in for a day and a night with two
other ducks, and then the three of them were turned out
into the farmyard together. In a few days it was back
in the farmyard of its original owner.

A farmer once sold a young pig to another farmer,
who lived across a lake from him. When delivering the
pig, the farmer took it in a wagon and drove around the
lake, a distance of about seven miles. The next morning the little pig was found back with his mother. It
was believed that he could not have made the journey
around the lake, but must have swum across the lake,
a distance of one mile.

Two young men mining in the Colorado desert of
California caught two desert tortoises, marked them by
boring holes in the margin of their shells, and carried
them with them when they visited their home in San
Bernardino, about 150 miles distant. They carried the
tortoises in a bag on the back of a mule. On arriving
in San Bernardino, the reptiles were turned loose. One
morning one of them was missing.

Several weeks later the young men set out on their
return journey to their mine, traveling by horse. About
halfway back, at the summit of Morongo Pass, they
found the missing tortoise, headed toward his home.
There wasn't any doubt about its being the same tortoise,
for it had the hole in its shell and other markings which
they had made. How did the little fellow find his way?

A French scientist wondered if wasps could find
their way back home, so caught a dozen of them, painted

their abdomens with white paint, put them in a cardboard container and took them two miles from their
nest. When he let them out they flew in different directions.

Five hours afterward, he found five of the painted
wasps back at their nest again, and a little later the other
seven returned also.

God has created all these dumb creatures. He has
placed in their hearts a love for home, and has given
them what we often call instinct, which helps them to do
things which we as human beings would have difficulty
in doing.

The same God who taught the honeybee how to make
honey from the flowers; who has given the oriole the
ability to build its wonderful nest; who guides these wild
creatures in their travels about our earth, has created us
and knows all about us. If perchance we happen to get
off the right road, will He not also help us to get back to
the straight path again? Will He not guide us back to
"our Father's house"? Of course, He will, if we will
permit Him.

The world would be a terrible place without friendship.

A Real Friend

FROM olden times comes the story of two young men who were very dear friends. They worked together, they played together, and they loved each other as much as if they were real brothers. Their names were Damon and Pythias.

One day Pythias did something that displeased the king, and this hard-hearted ruler gave orders that the boy should be put to death. The king put Pythias in prison, where he was to wait until the day of his execution.

He was a home boy. He loved his father and mother. So he sent word to the king, asking if he might be permitted to go home to bid them good-by.

"Why should I let you go?" asked the king. "If I should do so, you might run away. You would not come back."

Pythias tried to think of something he might do or say that would prove to the king that he would come back after he had said good-by to his parents. He and Damon talked it over. Finally Damon suggested a plan. "I will go to prison in your place and stay there until you return."

So Pythias said to the king, "I have a very dear friend who will stay in prison in my place."

"But," said the king to Damon, "I don't think Pythias will ever come back."

"Oh, yes, he will come back," said Damon. "He is honest and true. If he does not return, I will die in his place."

It was hard for a hard-hearted, selfish king to believe that one man would offer to die for another, but he let Pythias go home to bid his parents good-by, and sent Damon to prison.

The two boys hugged each other as they parted, and Pythias said to his friend, "Don't fear, Damon; I shall be back in plenty of time. I will not disappoint you."

The days dragged by for Damon, and to Pythias they seemed all too short. Finally the day on which Pythias was to die came, but he hadn't returned. The hour arrived, and the king and his soldiers came to the prison and led Damon out to die.

Just in time to save Damon from death, Pythias came running up. The ship on which he sailed had been wrecked and he had been delayed. He managed to reach shore, and then hurried as fast as he could on foot to save his friend, who had been good enough to go to prison for him. He was all out of breath. He feared he would be too late to save Damon.

The king was surprised to see him. He could not believe his eyes. He said, "Here is that foolish Pythias! I allowed him to go home to say good-by to his parents before he died. He promised he would return, but I did not think he would. But sure enough, here he is!"

The king called the young man to him. "Pythias, why did you come back to die, when you might have lived and been a free man by staying away?"

"But did I not say that I would come back?" said the boy. "I hurried as fast as I could, for I feared poor Damon would have to die in my place."

The king's heart was touched. Never had he seen such loyalty, such honesty, such devotion of one boy to another.

"Pythias shall live," he said, "and Damon shall go free also. Such true friends are worth more than my kingdom."

There is no greater treasure in the world than true friends. They are worth more to you than all the money in the world. Make friends, as many as you can. But remember, to have friends you must be friendly—you must be a friend.

Shep was a devoted friend to his master.

Only a Dog

SHEP, to most people, was "only a dog," a furry, good-natured collie. But to Mr. McMahon, a lonely laborer, he was a chum, a pal, a friend—yes, a part of his life. When home from work, this man and his dog were inseparable, and they spent many happy hours together.

One day Mr. McMahon fell down a flight of stairs and seriously injured his head. An ambulance called to take him to the hospital. Shep squeezed into the ambulance, and cuddled up as close as possible to his master, whining, and licking the man's face as if he knew something was wrong, and he wanted to encourage his friend.

As Mr. McMahon was carried from the ambulance into the hospital, Shep kept close beside him. The man was wheeled along the corridor and into a waiting elevator. Shep tried to get in too, but a man in white said, "No dogs allowed." It was hard for McMahon to be separated from his pal. He saw the look in Shep's eyes, and leaning forward stroked the dog's head and whispered to him, "It's all right, Shep, old pal. I'll be back soon. You wait for me here."

That changed the expression in the dog's eyes. He had heard that command before when his master had gone into some building or some home where dogs could not go. So Shep settled down by the elevator to wait patiently for his master's return.

I wish I could tell you that McMahon did come back and that he and Shep lived together happily ever after. But he didn't come back—he died the next day, and was carried out through another entrance to the undertakers. Shep didn't know what had happened to his friend. He knew that he had said, "Wait here for me, Shep. I'll come back," and his master had never failed him. He must wait! Each time the elevator reached that floor, the dog was ready to spring forward to meet his master.

For more than ten years Shep waited at the elevator for the return of McMahon. The nurses arranged a nice soft mat for him, and brought him food and water. Shep made friends with doctors, nurses, and visitors. They coaxed him out now and then for exercise and fresh air, but he was always anxious to get back to his post of waiting. He must not fail his master. For ten long years he kept watch for a friend who never returned. And the sad part of the story is that no one could explain to him just what had happened. Only a dog, yes, just a dog! But where would one find truer loyalty and devotion?

Here is another true story about a faithful dog.

Mr. Warren of Beaverton, Ontario, went to a nearby city hospital for an operation. Besides his family, he left at home a seven-year-old collie dog named Lassie. As soon as Mr. Warren left home, the animal refused to eat, and day by day grew weaker. Mrs. Warren didn't know what to do. She coaxed and pleaded. She bought special food for the dog, but Lassie would not taste a bite of it. In desperation she called her husband by telephone and told him of her problem.

"Put her to the phone," said Mr. Warren.

Mrs. Warren put the receiver to the dog's ear and Mr. Warren talked to her. As soon as she heard his voice she began to bark excitedly, and from that time on ate her meals regularly, and was soon her old self.

In Tonawanda, New York, two mongrel dogs had played together on the street most of the afternoon. Toward evening a car ran over the smaller of the two and killed him. That night people passing by saw Blackie, the other dog, sitting beside his dead chum. They passed on, for it was "only a dog." The next day Blackie still sat guarding his dead friend. It was snowing and a cold wind was blowing from the north, but for three days and nights the dog kept up his lonely vigil, until Humane Society officers came and removed him and buried his friend.

In a little homestead shack out near Rimbey, Alberta, lived a sixty-one-year-old man named Thomas Wilson and his dog. Mr. Wilson went to the post-office one cold winter day, and on the way home fell by the roadside, and died in a short time from exhaustion and exposure. When found, his little dog was standing guard over him. He refused to leave his master, and followed the body into town, where he watched over the body at the funeral parlor. Faithful in life and faithful in death!

Albert Payson Terhune has told a story about a dog of his, one named Sunnybank Jean. She had a puppy named Jock, which seemed very dear to her heart. Her affections continued long after the pup was weaned, which is quite unusual. Whenever she got a choice morsel, she saved all or part of it for Jock. Every day she washed him from head to toe. It was quite a task, for it all had to be done with her tongue. Wherever one was seen, the other was sure to be near. They were inseparable.

Jock fell ill with distemper and had to be isolated. The mother refused to eat. When Jock died, Jean was let out of her kennel, and she immediately began to hunt and search for her puppy. She barked, for Jock had always responded to her call. She sniffed over every foot of ground on the place. At last she found the spot where he had been buried. Then she came running to her master, Mr. Terhune, caught hold of his clothing with her teeth, and led him to the spot. She lay down beside the little mound of earth, with a look of hope in her eyes. She seemed to be saying, "He is here, he may come back sometime. I'd better wait."

Day after day for months and years she made her way to Jock's grave, where she spent hours of hopeful waiting. It is difficult to tell how long she would have continued this, but on a return trip one day she was run over by a car, and thus her life ended.

A man by the name of Wilson moved from Philadelphia to California, leaving behind a big brown collie named Jack. The dog refused to stay at his new home, and one day was found lying on the porch of the house his master had vacated. At a certain time every afternoon he made his way to the station to meet the train on which his master had been accustomed to come home. It had been a habit with him to meet Mr. Wilson each day when he came from work. Now he met the train, scanned every face, and, when his master did not come, returned dejectedly to the porch. He forgot about food; he would not eat. His only thought seemed to be of his master. He didn't know, of course, that he was hundreds of miles away in California. He became only skin and bones, and it was plain to be seen that he was dying of sorrow and loneliness.

A kind-hearted neighbor, who just couldn't stand to see the dog suffer, telegraphed the story to Wilson, who took the first train to Philadelphia. He boarded the train out to his old home, and was happy to find Jack there waiting for him. We will let Mr. Wilson tell just what happened:

"Jack gave a scream of unbelievable rapture and threw himself bodily on me, sobbing as a child might sob. He shivered all over as if he had a chill. And I? Well, I blew my nose hard and did a lot of fast winking. And I made a mighty resolve then and there that Jack and I never would be separated again as long as he should live."

Who wouldn't travel across the continent for such a friend?

On a farm in Northern Ontario a mother, alone with her two children, was stricken by serious illness. They had no telephone and the children were too small to send for help. She scribbled on a scrap of paper the one word, "Doctor," and tied it around the dog's neck. At her command the mongrel dog rushed off to a neighbor's house, and help soon arrived.

Most of you who read these lines have had dog friends, and know how true and faithful they are. It is often said that the dog is one of man's best friends. Many, many more stories might be told to prove this, but it is unnecessary.

Almost every animal known has been tamed by man. Grey Owl, a well-known naturalist, who lived for years in the Northwest, has made friends of the deer and the beavers living near his home. The beavers are very shy creatures, but they have become so well acquainted with him that they come to him for food and eat from his hands. Uncle Jack Miner says it is not the animals that are wild, but man.

Jiggs and Maggie

YOU WOULD hardly believe that a mother bird would leave her little ones to die for want of food and water, would you? But I know one mother pigeon who did that very thing. Maybe she was not to blame, though. I don't think she was.

This mother had been sitting for some days on two pretty white eggs. One morning we found two fuzzy yellow babies in the nest, and she seemed to be very proud of these homely little birds. It was too bad that they happened to be hatched just when we were moving. When the furniture had all been moved, we took the mother and her baby pigeons to their new home. A nice nest had been fixed for them in a corner of the garage. But the mother left those baby birds and went back to the old nest. We could not persuade her to stay and care for them.

We couldn't see the little fellows starve, so decided we would try to raise them ourselves. We soaked whole-wheat bread and grain, and fed it to them. They didn't know the first thing about eating, so we just opened their mouths and pushed the food in. They would eat and eat and eat, until their little crops would stick out like golf balls. When they were satisfied, they would settle down in their nest, contented, and usually go off to sleep. It was in the cool season of the year, so we had to keep them in the kitchen.

Whenever they became hungry, they would beg and cry for something to eat. When I got up in the morning, they gave me no peace until I had given them their breakfast. We took them up in our hands and fed them several times a day. Every day they grew larger, and soon the feathers began to appear. In just a short time they were all feathered out, and we took them to their house out in the garage.

Still we had to feed them, although by this time they had learned to take the food from our hands. Every time we went out of the house they expected attention of some kind. When they learned to fly, they would fly on our heads or shoulders and beg for something to eat. And if we did not go out, they would come to the window and beg for food or for a drink of water. We named them Jiggs and Maggie.

One evening when we came home, we found Jiggs in the house alone, and Maggie was missing. We looked overhead in the garage; we searched in the tree in the back yard; we hunted every place where we thought a bird might be. But we had to go to bed without finding her. The next morning we were up early to hunt some more. We inquired of the neighbors, but they had not seen her. Poor Jiggs was lonesome, and acted very strange.

That day our neighbor decided he would clean out his furnace and the pipes. When he took the pipes down, he heard a fluttering in the chimney, and there, covered with soot, he found a bird. At first he thought it might be a crow, but when he got it out in the light, he found it was Maggie. Weren't we happy to find her again! And wasn't it lucky for her that this man happened to clean his furnace pipes that day? She would have died there in the soot from hunger and thirst.

We brought her home, and gave her a bath in warm, soapy water. She really enjoyed it, for long before this

our pets had learned to take their baths regularly. Jiggs
was too happy to express his feelings, unless he said it
in bird language. He sat watching her preening her
feathers in the sun after her bath. Soon she was dry,
and feeling fine. We couldn't tell what Jiggs was saying, but he did a lot of talking.

They have raised several little families of their own,
but none of them are as tame and friendly as are Jiggs
and Maggie. They are the nicest pigeons we have ever
seen. We call them just as we call our dog, and they
come as readily. We love them, and they seem to know
it.

Don't Rope Those Calves, Son

AS THE father mounted his horse and rode off toward the range, he shouted to his young son Alex, "Son, don't you try to rope any of those range calves."

The boy was in the corral, trying to rope a post which stood some feet from him. His father had seen him practicing in this fashion before, and noticed that he was getting better at it every day. He knew there would be the temptation for the boy to rope something alive—a calf or a cow, or perhaps a horse. The father knew, too, that if the boy roped a calf which happened to have a mother nearby, there might be trouble.

Alex lived on a large cattle ranch in the West. To him life meant wide-open plains covered with hundreds of cows, calves, horses, and cowboys.

His life from babyhood had been spent out in the open. He had learned to ride a horse almost as soon as he learned to walk, so while now only a boy, he was about as much at home in the saddle as he would be on a kitchen chair.

The cowboys were his heroes. He longed for the day to come when he could ride the range with them, when he could herd and rope cows, and have a part in the big roundups. He begged his father to get him a big cowboy hat and a pair of Angora chaps.

There wasn't much fun in roping stones and posts and such things. So one day when Alex was alone out on the plains, astride his favorite horse, he decided that he was old enough now to do a little roping for himself. He found a number of wild longhorn cattle grazing.

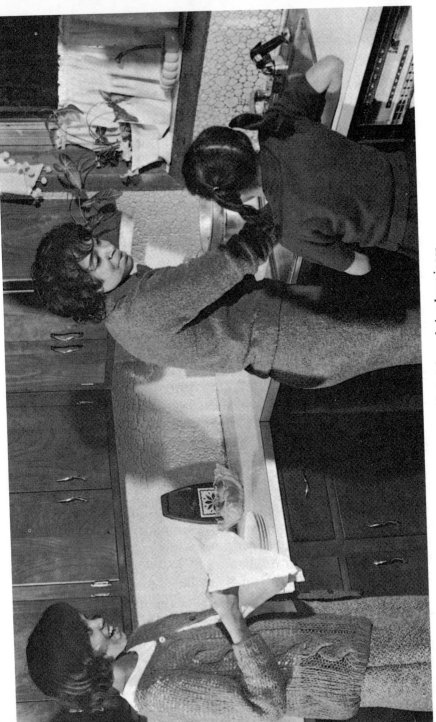

Obedience and helpfulness bring happiness.

Their calves were feeding with them. Alex rode up close to them, coiled the rope carefully in his hand, and wrapped one end of it a couple of times around the saddle horn.

He picked out a calf as a target, and threw the rope. He had aimed well, for it fell over the calf, and of course it started to run. The rope tightened as he pulled on it, and soon the little animal was squirming and struggling to free itself, all the while bawling frantically. It attracted the attention of its mother, and she came to its rescue. The other wild longhorns joined her, and they stampeded toward the pony and Alex. The pony had been on the range a long time and knew just what this meant. It knew it was time to be moving, and it moved quickly, speeding away in the direction of the river.

The rope on the horn of the saddle was loose and pulled off easily. Alex tried to stop the horse, but there was no stopping it, for those longhorn cattle were not far behind. Soon they neared the river bank, and the boy felt sure the horse would stop there. But it did not. Although it was a number of feet from the bank down to the water, the pony made one mad jump and landed well out in the swollen river. The river was swift and the water deep. Alex hung on for dear life while the pony was carried along down stream by the current. After a time she managed to get to the bank and struggled up out of the water.

It was an exciting ride—the kind Alex had heard the cowboys tell about. But he felt he didn't care for another one just like it. When he had gotten back on the plains, he did some thinking. Of course, he thought of what his father had told him, "Don't rope any of those calves, son." And he resolved that never again would he disobey his father, for it had almost cost him his life.

Alex was fortunate. Not every one who has dis-
obeyed has fared so well. There is always a price to pay
for disobedience. It is well to learn this early in life,
for it may save us embarrassment and suffering.

In a cemetery which I have occasion to visit now and
then there is a little tombstone which reminds me, each
time I see it, of the fruits of disobedience.

At one time we lived next door to an aunt of mine.
She had a little boy named Everett, who was about
twelve years old. One day she sent him to the city,
which was about a mile and a half from their home. He
had to walk the three miles. There were several errands
to attend to in the city, one of which was to mail a letter
that he carried in his pocket. He returned home, somewhat tired from his walk.

"Did you mail that letter, Everett?" his mother
asked.

He felt in his pocket. It was still there.

"You must go right back to the post office with it,"
said his mother. "It is important that it go out tonight."

There was a short cut to town. One could walk up
the railroad track and save at least a half mile. There
was a well worn path out on the right of way, so there
was little danger. But the boys of the community had
formed the habit of hopping slow-moving freights
which traveled over this line.

Everett asked if he might go up the railroad track
and save a lot of time and walking. His mother said
he might, "But," she warned, "don't you ever attempt
to hop a train, son. You might be run over."

The little fellow hurried off on his errand. As he
trudged along the railroad a freight came chugging by.

It was not moving very fast, and he was so tired that he was tempted to jump on and ride into the city. He felt sure that he could get on all right, for the boys did it every day and none of them seemed to get hurt. So he attempted to hop on one of the freight cars. But he misjudged the speed, and was pulled down along the side of the train. His tired little legs seemed out of control, and rolled right under the car.

Section men picked him up a few minutes later, and hurried him to a doctor. I reached him in just a little while and found him lying on the doctor's table, chewing his gum. He had lost so much blood, that his life slowly ebbed away. I was with him through the long night, and he talked much of the mistake he had made in disobeying his mother. With him, disobedience was costly indeed.

Some disobey the laws of the land. Sooner or later they are caught in their disobedience and must pay the price. Maybe the sentence is to go to jail for a few months, maybe to the penitentiary for years, and for some it is the electric chair or the gallows.

Some disobey the laws of health. They eat things they know will hurt them. They smoke and drink just to be like others, even though they know it is harmful. The penalty is stomach trouble, bad nerves, cancer, and many other ailments.

For every violation of law, whether it be God's law or man's, there is a penalty. The rule is—obey or pay.

To its family, a baby is one of the most important things in the world.

Just Little Things

"THERE are no little things," says Bruce Barton. You might be interested in the whole quotation. Here it is: "Sometimes when I consider what tremendous consequences come from little things—a chance word, a tap on the shoulder, or a penny dropped on a newsstand—I am tempted to think . . . there are no little things."

A few months ago a friend was driving me around in the city of Chicago. Somewhere on the south side, I have forgotten the street and number, he showed me where the great Chicago fire started some years ago. Some one was out milking after dark, and the cow kicked over the lantern. Just a small kerosene lantern it was too—but it started that great fire which left thousands homeless and reduced a great city to just a smoldering heap.

The French submarine *Lutin* was at one time maneuvering off the coast of Tunis. Time after time it descended into the depths and returned safely to the surface with its proud crew. But joy turned to consternation when it remained beneath the surface longer than was expected. Anxiously the spectators on other vessels near by looked for some sign of its return. Then rescue attempts were feverishly begun. The French Government did everything within its power, but weeks slipped by before the submarine was raised to the surface, and by that time every man of her crew was found dead. Investigations were begun to find the cause of the disaster. A tiny pebble was found in one of the valves. It was just a small stone, but it had prevented the valve from operating properly, and caused the loss of the submarine and its entire crew.

A young lawyer, just out of school, settled in a town to practice law. There were already too many successful lawyers in the vicinity, and some one asked him if he thought he would make a living. "I may get a little practice," he replied.

"Yes," the questioner replied, "you may, but it will be very little."

"Then," said the young man, "I shall do that well."

The destiny of men and nations really hinges on the little things of life. In Luke 16:10 we read, "He that is faithful in that which is least is faithful also in much: and he that is unjust in the least is unjust also in much."

A bishop, traveling through the country, came to a crossroads settlement of a few houses, among which was a neat little shoe shop owned by an old man, who seemed busy, happy and prosperous. The clergyman, who was interested in finding odd characters in unheard-of places, stopped for a chat.

"My friend," said the bishop, "You seem to be busy and happy. I should not think a shoe shop would be very prosperous in such an out-of-the-way place."

Another gentleman, who happened to be in the little shop, spoke up before the old shoemaker had a chance to answer, and said: "Cato has a monopoly on the shoe mending business in this district. No one else gets any shoe repairing in these parts."

"How do you account for that, Cato?" asked the bishop. "Why does all the shoe repair work come here? People must have to come a long way to bring their shoes to you. What is the explanation?"

"I guess there is no secret about it, mister," said Cato. "It's only little patches put on with little stitches or tiny nails. But when I take a stitch, it is a stitch; and when I drive a nail, it is there to stay."

In other words it was another case of little things well done.

Dr. L. K. Hisberg says Napoleon's poor penmanship had much to do with his defeat at Waterloo. He scrawled a note to his lieutenant, Grouchy, intending to say, "The battle is on." And Grouchy couldn't make out the awful penmanship. He deciphered it to be, "The battle is won," so with his thousands of trained veterans he leisurely made his way to Waterloo, only to find that Napoleon had been defeated. How many there are who have been defeated because of carelessness in the little things.

Just a little comma, if put in the wrong place in a sentence, may change the meaning entirely. A buyer for a large business house wired his firm to inquire if he should buy certain merchandise. They replied, "No, price too high." He interpreted it to read, "No price too high," and bought the goods in question. It cost his firm thousands of dollars. A new tariff bill intended to encourage the cultivation of certain foreign fruit plants of high quality, was introduced to the government. It was passed, and these fruit trees were to be admitted free. The printer got a comma out of place and it read, "Foreign fruit, plants, etc., are to be admitted free." Because a comma was inserted between fruit and plants the government lost thousands of dollars in revenue.

A member of a school board decided to visit the school which he, as a trustee, was helping to manage. On entering the room, he found a class in grammar at

The helpless baby of today may be the great person of tomorrow.

the board. One of the boys was having trouble with his
punctuation. The teacher rather chided the boy because
he couldn't punctuate the sentence correctly. The visi-
tor tried to encourage the lad. "Don't be discouraged,
son," he said. "Those commas don't matter a great deal."
Thereupon the teacher asked the boy to write this
sentence on the board: "The president of the school
board says the teacher is a fool." "Now my boy," said
the teacher, "please put a comma after board and one

after teacher." The sentence then read, "The president of the school board, says the teacher, is a fool."

The board member saw the point.

One little misplaced comma in the Bible has caused no end of discussion, and has really brought a great difference of opinion among Christian people as to the condition of man after death. You will find the text in Luke 23:43. Jesus, while hanging on the cross, spoke to the penitent thief. In the English Bible His statement is punctuated as follows: "Verily I say unto thee, To day shalt thou be with Me in Paradise." Many believe the comma in this sentence is misplaced and that the verse should read, "Verily I say unto thee today, Thou shalt be with Me in Paradise." The placing of that little comma makes a great deal of difference in the interpretation of the verse.

A famous painting by an old master, a work of art of fabulous worth, was ruined by a small hole in a tile roof. The painting had been carefully guarded, and the building in which it was kept was supposed to be secure. But a driving, beating rain from the east found its way through the imperfect tile, and the painting was ruined. Some workman had doubtless seen the flaw in the tile, but thought that it would not matter.

It is the "little foxes that spoil the vines," the "little leaks which sink a great ship." Little neglects in any life will sooner or later bring regrets.

One writer has said, "The little incidents of every day life often pass without our notice; but it is these things that shape the character."

I am not a prophet, but show me a boy or girl who is careful about the little things, who does not neglect the trifles, who keeps his promises, who is on time for appointments, who performs small tasks well, and I will show you a person who will succeed in life.

Most things of consequence in this world begin small and grow bigger. Great industries of today began in a small way, you will find, if you go back to their beginning. In the early 1890's C. W. Post went to Battle Creek, Michigan, and with a seventy-dollar investment began to make Postum Cereal. Today this mammoth organization sends its products to the ends of the earth.

Florence Nightingale began her nursing career by caring for a wounded collie dog.

A few decades ago a New England farm boy borrowed eighteen dollars from his father, and with the money bought a heifer. He killed and dressed the animal, and from an old covered wagon sold the meat from door to door in the quiet little village of Barnstable, Massachusetts. When he returned home that evening, the wagon was empty, and the young man had thirty-eight dollars in his pocket. He had made a profit of twenty dollars. That boy was Gustave F. Swift, and that was the beginning of the great Swift and Company.

In his book *Making Life a Masterpiece,* Mr. Marden illustrates the value of little things in a most interesting way. "On the floor of the gold working room in the United States Mint at Philadelphia," says he, "is a wooden lattice-work which is taken up when the floor is swept, and the fine particles of gold dust—valued at thousands of dollars yearly—are saved." He goes on to point out that those of us who wish to make the most of this life should have a "similar network to catch the raspings and parings of existence, those leavings of days and bits of hours which most people sweep into the waste of life."

Some years ago some well-meaning person thought he was doing Australia a favor by introducing a few rabbits into the country. Those few rabbits multiplied so rapidly that the country is overrun with the animals. Some other misguided individual thought he was doing as much for North America by introducing some house-sparrows into the United States. You know the end of the story.

Some one once asked why Paderewski was then the greatest of living pianists. The answer is not at all surprising—"Because more than any other, he lingers lovingly on beautiful details in the music he is playing."

A tall, stately giant of the forest, which had stood through the storms of centuries, crashed to earth one still summer day. Rings on its trunk were counted, and they revealed the fact that this great tree was growing when the Pilgrims landed at Plymouth Rock, yes, when Columbus came to North America. It was more than 500 years old. All those years it had withstood the blizzards of winter, and the hurricanes, the windstorms of summer. Scars showed that it had been struck by lightning a number of times. But why should such a giant crash to earth on a calm summer day?

The heart of the great tree was eaten away. A pair of tiny beetles had bored under the bark. They had worked and multiplied until there were colonies of black beetles working silently toward the heart of the tree. Finally, the life and fiber of the mighty giant were destroyed, and it crashed to earth. It had withstood the storms, the lightning, and the elements for centuries, but a tiny black beetle got into its heart and caused its ruin.

How many people have gone through life neglecting

the little things they might do well, and looking long-ingly for some great deed to be done. How many have withstood the real storms and tempests of temptation, and have fallen over some little sin. We aren't tempted to rob a bank, to murder some one, or to commit some great wrong. But it is so easy to yield to the "little" temptation.

A little word, a little smile, a warm hand clasp, a cup of cold water, may cheer some struggling pilgrim along life's way. A frown, an unkind criticism, may bring discouragement.

If a little sin should ruin your life and keep you out of heaven, it would really not be a little sin after all.

Life's Little Things

The cooing of the baby,
  The perfume of the flowers,
The song of happy birds that sing,
  Within their shady bowers;
The tinting of the daisies,
  The twilight's purple glow—
We deem them little things indeed
  In life's great onward flow!

The whispered word of courage,
The grip of friendship's hand
The smile that casts its kindly light
  Across life's desert sand,
The hope that cheers the spirit
  When sorrow spreads its wings—
Ah, yes, how sadly often here,
  We deem them little things.

But if they passed forever
  From out the school of life,
And if they left no gleam to cheer
  Amid the darkened strife,
The bitter loss would stun us,
  And poison joy's sweet springs,
O careless heart, remember then,
  And prize life's little things.
                    —*Robert Hare.*

Dr. Ralph J. Bunche is an important person at the United Nations.

From "Pig Boy" to Peacemaker

T HE name of Ralph J. Bunche has been stamped so clearly on the thinking of American people that he is today considered an outstanding statesman. In one sphere, at least, that of dealing with quick tempers and hostile groups, he has seldom been equaled.

Ralph Bunche was born in Detroit, Michigan, August 7, 1904, the son of a not-too-well-off barber. As the family was large, Ralph, his parents, his grandmother, and her four other grown children all lived under the same roof.

The family was very poor. During the summer Ralph and his sister always went barefoot. They saved their shoes for the fall when they re-entered school. Ralph early learned the value of money—even a few pennies served to bring him great pleasure. A penny spent for candy would buy enjoyment for all day. Most of his boyhood amusements cost him nothing at all.

Always, endlessly he had to work. At the age of seven he ran errands for a grocery store and sold newspapers on a street corner. Later, after the family moved to Los Angeles, he worked during vacation periods as a house servant in wealthy homes or as a kitchen boy in large hotels. At another time he was a delivery boy for a Los Angeles newspaper, riding on his bicycle afternoons picking up advertising copy. At the same plant he got a better job as "pig boy" in a composing room. This meant that he was responsible for keeping the linotype machines supplied with lead. This hard work continued from five-thirty in the afternoon until one o'clock

in the morning. When he got home, it would be nearly
two o'clock, and he would fall exhausted on his bed.
After about six hours of sleep, with very little opportunity to study or to look after home duties, he had to
rush for school.

When he came to college, he had to think of other
devices by which he could earn money. Ralph and one of
his college chums hit upon an idea. They bought a
Model T Ford for twenty-five dollars, made it bulge
with mops, buckets, and brooms, and offered their com-
bined services to local stores and lunchrooms as a clean-
up crew. The idea caught on, and beginning at six
o'clock each morning, they mopped and polished about
half a dozen business shops, and were back in college for
the nine o'clock classes. During summer vacations he
worked as a bus boy and petty officers' messman on a
ship. This usually brought three hundred dollars.

In his schoolwork, Ralph's grades were of such
quality that he won scholarships for three years. Besides his usual round of manual work and studies, he
worked on the college daily paper, was one of the editors
of the yearbook, and was president of the debating society.

When graduated from college in 1927, he received
a scholarship to do advanced work at Harvard University. His was an exuberant feeling. But not for long.
What he had not realized was that the Harvard appointment covered merely tuition costs. There was no money
for railroad fare. And even if he could gather that
money, there was nothing to apply on room, board, and
other incidentals.

Just then he received unexpected help. A generous
woman had taken an interest in him. When she learned

of his problem, she called a meeting of her club. The members decided to hold a benefit "to send our Ralph to Harvard." The club members raised one thousand dollars, and off he set for Cambridge, Massachusetts.

He had with him a letter from a friend in Los Angeles who operated a bookshop. This was addressed to the manager of a bookstore in the main section of Cambridge. The letter requested the book dealer to give Ralph a discount on his textbooks. But the dealer could not see very well, and he assumed that the letter carried a different message. "If you're looking for a job," he said, "I'll hire you."

Ralph was at work the following day. He now had nearly eight hundred dollars left from the club gift, and he had steady employment.

He finally received the doctor of philosophy degree in political science. He was the first Negro to be so honored. Financed by the Rosenwald Fund and the Social Science Research Council, he made extended field trips. In South Africa, he formed a marvelous friendship with the people, and this prepared the way for later opportunities that were offered him. He was selected during World War II as chief of the Africa section of the Office of Strategic Services.

One surprise now followed another in his many appointments to new and exciting work. He was transferred to the State Department. He was the first Negro to hold a "desk job" in that department. He was an adviser at Dumbarton Oaks, at the first U.N. session held in San Francisco, and at later meetings of the Council of Foreign ministers, and the U.N. General Assembly. Eventually he went to work with the U.N. as director of the trusteeship division.

When fighting broke out in the Holy Land between the Arabs and the Jews, Dr. Bunche was chosen to go along with Count Folke Bernadotte, who was appointed as mediator by Trygve Lie. Count Bernadotte was assassinated before the mission was scarcely under way, and Dr. Bunche took over these responsibilities. For the monumental achievement in settling the Palestine dispute, Dr. Bunche is now known the world over.

His formula for success is a generous mixture of determination and endless hard work. His secretary, Doreen Daughton, is responsible for the observation that she "never once saw him lose his temper."

His grandmother, a tiny woman of vibrant spirit and strong conviction, provided him with what amounts to his guiding philosophy for living. "Your color," she counseled, "has nothing to do with your worth. You are potentially as good as anyone. How good you may prove to be will have no relation to your color, but with what is in your heart and head. The right to be treated as an equal by all other men is man's birthright. Never permit anyone to treat you otherwise. Who, indeed, is a better American, a better protector of the American heritage, than he who demands the fullest measure of respect for those cardinal principles on which our society is reared? . . .

"There will be many and great obstacles in your path, and this is the way of life. But only weaklings give up in the face of obstacles. Be honest and frank with yourself and the world at all times. Never compromise what you know to be the right. Never pick a fight, but never run from one if your principles are at stake. Go out into the world with your head high, and keep it high at all times."

Conscience Did It

ONE FINE morning, when the mail was being opened in the city offices of Long Beach, California, there was found one unusual letter from Regina, Saskatchewan, hundreds of miles to the north, across the Canadian border. Out of that letter rolled a bright, shiny dime, and there was a brief letter of explanation. It read: "I once had a ride on a Long Beach street car. I did not pay my fare. I am sending it to you with interest."

The money went to the city's "conscience fund."

The Chicago chief of police one day received a letter containing $4.61 from some one in New Orleans. The man explained that twenty-nine years before he had stolen a penny on a Chicago street car, and later stole fifty cents from his mother. He was returning what he had stolen with interest.

Conscience did it. The man in Regina, Saskatchewan, just couldn't rest until he had paid for the trolley ride, and the man in New Orleans got tired of something telling him day after day that he ought to pay back that money he had taken.

This thing we call conscience is peculiar, isn't it? No one has ever seen a conscience, and it would be hard to explain just what it is and how it works. But we each have one, and should be thankful we have. An old Indian, when asked about his conscience, said it was "a three-cornered something which pricks me whenever I turn from the right way."

When I was a boy in my teens, a gentleman who lived

near us asked me to come and spade his garden. He said
that he would give me fifty cents a day. I was anxious to
make some money, and reported for work early the next
morning. He gave me a spading fork and set me to
work. It was hard work, but fifty cents was a lot of
money to me.

In the middle of the morning I turned up a coin with
one of the forkfuls of earth. I quickly tucked it away
in my pocket. I thought sure it must be a half dollar,
and if it were I would have two half dollars for that
day's work. But my conscience said, "That is not your
money. It is Mr. Long's, for you found it in his garden.
You had better give it to him."

I tried to argue with my conscience that I had found
it and that it was mine. But all morning long that conscience kept telling me it would not be right for me to
keep the money. So I took it to Mr. Long and told
him I had dug it up in the garden. He could see that,
for it looked as if it had been in the earth for a long time.
"I don't think it is mine," he said, "so you may have it."
At noon I gave it a good cleaning and polishing, and,
sure enough, it was a real half dollar. So I had two half
dollars for my work that day, and I was happy. If I
had not told Mr. Long about this, I would have been miserable, for my conscience would have told me over and
over again that I had done wrong.

When working in a large woolen mill in New York
City, a young man was persuaded to sell a bolt of cloth
worth $110, which belonged to his employer. For ten
years his conscience bothered him. It told him about
his wrong doing day after day. So at the end of that
time, he could stand it no longer. He sent his former
employer a check for $110.

When the mail was being opened one morning in the government offices in Ottawa, there was found a short letter of unusual interest, addressed to the premier. Here is the letter: "During the war I received goods unlawfully, belonging to the government, valued at just over one dollar. For so doing I enclose three dollars, and wish to express my regret to those concerned and to acknowledge my sin against Almighty God."

It wasn't a large amount, but the paying of it brought peace to a troubled conscience.

Another letter which came to this same office read, "Through the guidance of God, I have been led to send you this money." In some way this young lady had defrauded the government, so sent a check for $34.53.

The street railway company of New York City once received a letter containing twenty cents in stamps. It came from Virginia and was to pay for a ride on their street car forty-five years before, when the cars were being drawn by horses. The rider had been "just a boy," and the fare only five cents. But he just didn't feel right until he had paid for the ride, so he sent along twenty cents in stamps, which paid for the ride with interest.

Another soldier wrote to his government: "While in service during 1918-20 I stole equipment and clothing to the amount, as near as I can tell, of about fifty dollars. Since that time God has come into my life, and I am going back over my tracks and making every wrong right that I possibly can. Enclosed find check for same, and by His grace I hope nothing of its kind will have to be repeated."

A large hotel received a dollar bill and a note with no name signed. The note read, "To ease my conscience for the taking of two linen towels twenty years ago."

A lady in Indiana was very much surprised to find in her mail one day a letter from some one she did not know. It contained a dollar bill, and explained that when a boy of thirteen, the sender had stolen a watermelon from this lady's father. The man whose melon

School is worthless if a boy or girl cheats in his studies.

patch the boy had entered was dead, so the money was sent to his daughter. "I am on my way to heaven," the man wrote, "and have run up against that melon. It has grown so large I cannot get over it. Please forgive and forget."

Edna Russell has written a lovely poem about this peculiar something which we all have in our hearts. She says:

"I have a little conscience
That lives inside of me;
It certainly is a nuisance
When bad I want to be.

"It talks to me and bothers me,
And sometimes I can't sleep.
It keeps me out of trouble,
When its advice I keep.

"It's nice to have a conscience,
And listen to its voice;
For between right and wrong
It lets me have my choice."

We should be thankful that our Maker has given this guide to help us in choosing the right way, and to warn us if we get on the wrong path. One cannot get away from it, but it does talk to us more faintly if we fail to listen to its voice.

A student who had cheated in examinations in algebra tried to still the voice of conscience. But she could get no peace. She left school, and years rolled by; she traveled across the seas, but still that small voice talked to her about her dishonesty in school. And because of this little voice, her teacher, who had almost forgotten the girl, received this letter, sent from Africa: "Twenty-five years ago I was in your algebra class, and I cheated in an examination. It has troubled me ever since. I have decided that my peace of mind is worth more than pride, and I am therefore making confession of my wrong. Please forgive me."

Two letters came to two different railroads in the city of Winnipeg in the same mail. They were from California, and each contained a check. The letters said, "I am sending this money in order to quiet my conscience." The letter to the Canadian National Railway contained twenty-seven dollars to pay for railway fare and interest from Gravelbourg to Moose Jaw. The letter to the Canadian Pacific Railway contained sixty-five dollars, and explained that the writer had taken a little boy all the way from Moose Jaw to Long Beach, California, without paying his fare. "Please forgive me," the writer said. This person's conscience, no doubt, had talked to her when she took the little boy on the train without paying. She knew she was doing wrong. But she wanted to save that much money. Her conscience still talked to her, and she could get no rest until she had paid the railway fare and made the wrong right.

No, you have never seen a conscience, and never will. But it is a wonderful something which God has placed in every human heart. If we listen to its voice, it is not likely that we shall go far astray. If we disobey it, or try to smother it, we are sure to have regrets. Let's keep it sensitive and in good working order.

The Little Protector

THE LITTLE boy was desperately in earnest. He marched straight into the store on that snowy morning. Up to the first clerk he went. "I want to see the 'prietor," said he.

The clerk almost smiled, but the little boy before her was so grave that she answered solemnly, "He is over at his desk."

The lad walked over to the man at the desk. Mr. Martin, the proprietor, turned around. "Good morning, little man. Did you want to see me?" he asked.

"Yes, sir. I want a coat for my mother. I can make fires and pay for it."

"Young man, what is your name?"

"Paul Johnson."

"Is your father living?"

"No, sir; he died when we lived in Louisville."

"How long have you lived here?"

"We haven't been here long. Mother was sick in Louisville, and the doctor told her to go away, and she would get well."

"Is she better?"

"Yes, sir. Last Sunday she wanted to go to church, but she didn't have a coat, and she cried. She didn't think I saw her, but I did. She says I am her little p'tector since father died. I can make fires and pay for the coat."

"But, little man, the store is steam-heated. I wonder if you could clean the snow off the walk."

"Yes, sir," Paul answered, quickly.

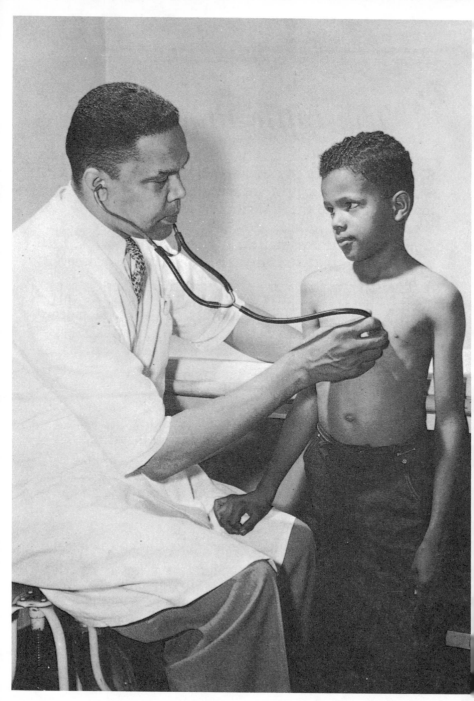

Paul felt bad when he became sick and could not work at the store.

"Very well. I'll write your mother a note and explain our bargain."

When the note was written, Mr. Martin arose. "Come, Paul, I will get the coat," he said. At the counter he paused. "How large is your mother, Paul?" he asked.

Paul glanced about him. " 'Bout as large as her," he said, pointing toward a lady clerk.

"Miss Smith, please see if this fits you," requested Mr. Martin. Paul's eyes were shining.

Miss Smith put on the coat and turned about for Paul to see it. "Do you like it?" she asked him.

"Yes, I do," he answered very emphatically.

The coat was marked thirty dollars, but kindhearted Mr. Martin said: "You may have it for twelve dollars, Paul."

"Take it to Pauline, and have her take the price tag off," he added to Miss Smith.

"When the snow stops falling, come and sweep off the walk," he said to Paul. "I will pay you a dollar each time you clean it. We shall soon have enough to pay for the coat."

"Yes, sir," answered Paul gravely. He took the bundle and trudged out into the snow.

When he reached home, his mother looked in surprise at his bundle. "Where have you been, dear?"

"I went to town, Mother," Paul answered. He put the note into her hand. She opened it, and read:

"Mrs. Johnson: This little man has bought a coat for you. He says he is your protector. For his sake keep the wrap and let him work to pay for it. It will be a great pleasure to him. He has the making of a fine man in him.—WILLIAM MARTIN."

Paul was astonished to see tears in his mother's eyes. He had thought that she would be so happy, but instead she was crying. She put her arm about him and kissed him. Then she put on the coat, and told him how pretty she thought it was.

When the snow stopped falling, Paul went down to the store and cleaned the front walk. He did not know that Mr. Martin's hired man swept it again, for the little arms were not strong enough to sweep it quite clean.

The days passed, and one morning Paul had a very sore throat.

"You mustn't get up today, dear," his mother said. When she brought his breakfast, she found him crying. "What is making you cry? Is your throat hurting much?" she inquired.

"No, Mama. Don't you see it is snowing, and I can't go and clean the walk?" cried Paul.

"Shall I write a note to Mr. Martin and explain why you are not there?"

"Yes, please, Mama. Who will take it?"

"I'll ask Bennie to leave it as he goes to school," replied Mrs. Johnson.

The note was written, and Bennie, a neighbor boy, promised to deliver it.

While Paul was eating his dinner, there was a knock at the door. Mrs. Johnson answered it, and ushered in Mr. Martin.

"How is the sick boy?" he asked. He crossed the room and sat by Paul. He patted the boy's cheek, and then turned to the mother. "Mrs. Johnson," he said, "my wife's mother is very old, but will not give up her home and live with us. She says she wants a home for her children to visit. She has recently lost a good housekeeper, and needs another. Since I met Paul the other day, I have been wondering if you would take the housekeeper's place. Mother would be glad to have you and Paul with her, and would make things easy for you, and pay you liberally."

"I shall be very glad to accept your offer, Mr. Martin. I am sorely in need of work. I taught in the public school in Louisville until my health failed. Since then I have had a hard struggle to get along," answered Mrs. Johnson.

"I will give you Mother's address. You can go out and arrange matters. Make haste and get well, little protector," said Mr. Martin, as he rose to go.

When he had gone, the mother put her arms about her boy. "You are my protector," she said. "You brought me a coat, and now you have helped me to get work."

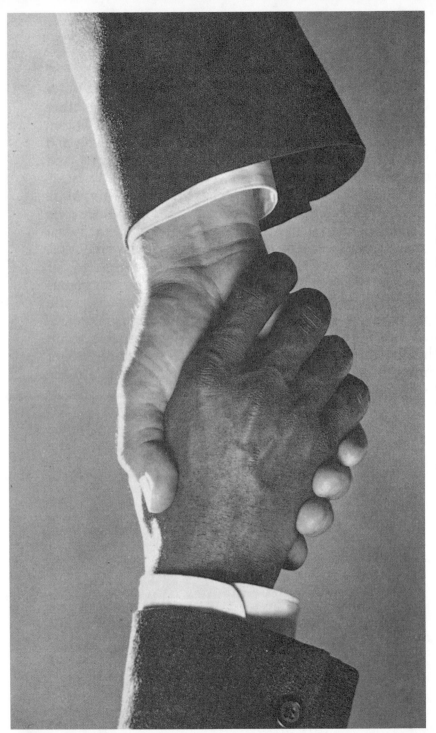

People's customs make most of them shake hands with their right hand.

Why and How

SOME years ago a young man by the name of O'Sullivan worked in a factory where there was much heavy machinery. The machines shook the building constantly. Since he had to stand on his feet all day, this constant jarring troubled him. One day he brought a piece of rubber matting to the factory and stood on it while he worked. This took away some of the jar. But some one took his mat. He thought it would be useless to bring another, for they would take that also. So he got two pieces of rubber and nailed them to the heels of his shoes. He was the inventor of rubber heels. He now has a factory and is perhaps the largest manufacturer of rubber heels in the world.

In England or Canada the word "peeler" or "bobbie" means a policeman. In the United States "cop" is more familiar. Sir Robert Peel was the man who first hired a force of men, dressed them in uniforms, and gave them the task of protecting the people and enforcing the laws. So policemen in some countries are called "bobbies" or "peelers."

Why are wedding rings worn on the third finger? Because many years ago people thought there was a separate vein which connected the third finger of the left hand with the heart. So when a young woman promised a young man her heart, he slipped a wedding ring on the third finger of the left hand. We know there is no particular connection between this one finger and the heart, but the custom still remains.

It has become a custom for a man and woman, when

they become married, to take a wedding trip, which we call their "honeymoon." Where could such a strange word have come from? It was the practice of the ancients to drink a certain kind of wine, made of honey, for thirty days after they were married, or for a moon after marriage. The moon has always been associated with lovers and their romances, and romance with marriage; so the moon or month after marriage has come to be called the "honeymoon."

We hear a great deal about jubilees these days. There are silver jubilees and diamond jubilees. Usually jubilees are held in commemoration of some great event. The word jubilee really comes from an old Hebrew word *jobil*, which in that language was a ram's horn. When any great event was proclaimed, it was usually announced by blowing a ram's horn, and thus these great events or celebrations came to be called jubilees.

"Why do people wear black or dress in mourning when some loved one dies? Hundreds of years ago, when some one died, the relatives feared that the ghost of the one who had died would return and do them harm. Hence they tried to disguise themselves so the returning ghost would not know them. At first they plastered their faces with mud, and later began to wear a black veil. And with the black veil came other black garments.

Hat tipping is a sign of courtesy. How did it originate? In olden times a warrior used to take off some of his armor or war trappings as a sign of respect or friendliness. But the knight of the Middle Ages was clad in a full armor made of metal. It was a job to get out of it. In the front of the helmet was a metal door or vizor which could be raised or opened when the warrior was not in battle. So it became a custom that when a knight should meet a lady, instead of taking off his armor, he merely lifted or opened the vizor as an act of courtesy. From vizor lifting we got our hat tipping.

Man used to wear a cloth around his neck, something like our mufflers. Some one tied his muffler into a neat knot. It looked quite dressy, and the modern necktie followed.

Most of us, early in life, wore a bib. It is a very useful article for a baby, for it protects the clothing and soaks up liquids which may fall on it. During its first months the baby "imbibes" or drinks its mother's milk. The word "bib" is no doubt a contraction of the term "imbibes," since the bib drinks in or soaks up liquids which fall on it.

Thimbles were first used in Europe during the Middle Ages, but they were not just the same as our thimbles today. They were made of leather and worn on the thumb; in those times they were called "thummels," and later came to be called thimbles.

In the far northern country of Iceland streams of water gushed or spouted from the earth in certain places. The word in that land which means to "gush" or to "rush forth," is *geysa*. So such fountains are called "geysers" in our land today.

When you go to a restaurant to eat, you are given a card on which is printed a list of the good things from which you may choose your meal. This we call a "menu." Duke Henry of Brunswick, when sitting at a feast with friends, was noticed to glance often at a long slip of paper. When asked by a friend what he was studying, he said the chef had drawn up for him a list of all the dishes, so his master might choose the things he liked the best.   The guests liked this idea, and the menu was soon being used in all parts of Europe.

In the olden days girls who were planning to be married spent a great deal of their time spinning and weaving linens and cloth.   From this cloth they made their wedding gowns and other articles which would be used in their new homes.   And since all the girls were so busy spinning, they were called "spinsters."   Thus unmarried women are still called by this name.

Do you know how the little bow got on the side of men's hats? History says that caps of the long, long ago were made the same size, but were equipped with laces on the right side so they could be adjusted to fit the owner's head.   Later the lace was replaced by a ribbon, and we still have the little bow of ribbon on our hats, even though hats are made to fit our heads today.

Before books were as common as they are today, persons fortunate enough to own such valuable possessions guarded them carefully, often chaining those containing a record of business transactions to the ledge of their office or home. Thus these books came to be called "ledgers."

Bright's disease was named after Richard Bright, an English physician, who died in 1858.

A man of the name of Macintosh discovered that he could make coats out of thin sheets of rubber and that these coats would keep off the rain.   People liked these new coats, and now almost every one has a raincoat.   To this day they are called "mackintoshes."

Do you know how rubber got its name?   In the year 1779 a man from England discovered that a piece of this queer, soft, spongy material would erase or rub out pencil marks.   And since it would rub out the marks, he called it "rubber," and it still carries the same name. In the old homes in England and Norway there was a long, narrow opening in the wall, the purpose of which was to let in the sunshine, but which, of course, let in the wind as well. In England this opening was called "windage," meaning "wind eye," or eye of the house, which let in the wind. Later they put glass in these "eyes" of the house, to keep out the wind, and the word "windage" finally became "window."

It was in the year 1622 that the first paper giving the happenings of the day appeared in England. On the top of this sheet were printed the points of the compass, to impress upon its readers the fact that the paper told of happenings in all parts of the world—the north, east, west, and south. Before long a wide-awake publisher arranged the first letters of these four words at the top of his sheet, and with them he formed the word "news." So these bulletins came to be called newspapers, and every publisher copied the idea.

One Sunday morning in the nineties a young clergyman stepped into a drug store, after his morning sermon, to eat a dish of ice cream. On this particular morning he decided to have something different than was his custom; so he asked the clerk to pour a little fruit syrup over his ice cream. He liked it so well that he asked for this same thing every Sunday morning, and called it his "Sunday." Thus ice cream with fruit syrup or chocolate poured over it came to be called "sundae."

The name "Quakers" was first given to the members of the Society of Friends by a justice named Bennet, because the founder of the Friends' religious body once admonished the magistrate that he "should quake at the word of God." So whenever he referred to this religious

sect, the justice called them "Quakers," and they still
go by this name today.

How did our common, everyday pen get its name?
After paper, such as we use now, had been invented, men
found it necessary to write with something very soft, so
it would not tear the paper. They began to use the feathers of geese and swans. The hard, stiff end or quill of
the feather was sharpened, and then split, so it would
hold the ink, and the feather part was used as a handle.
The Latin or Roman word for feather is *penna*. Since
they found that word a little long, they just shortened
it, and called it "pen." After these feathers or quills
were used for a time, the points wore off, and sometimes
they got broken. So every one kept a small knife handy
for sharpening pens. Now you see why small knives
are called "penknives."

Why do we always shake hands with our right hand?
This custom comes down to us from the time when
almost every one carried a sword or knife. If a person
met some one who he thought might not be a friend, he
immediately grasped his sword with his right hand,
ready to protect himself. But when he met a friend, he
extended the right hand to show that he did not have a
knife or sword in that hand. So we still follow the
custom of shaking hands, though we have long ago
ceased to carry swords.

When Professor Wilhelm Roentgen, of Germany,
discovered the X rays, he was not sure of their nature.
X has been used for many years to represent unknown
substances and quantities; so he just called the rays
"X rays."

The Poor Old Gander

WALTER, when only eight years old, went to spend the summer vacation with his grandfather and grandmother on the farm. He wasn't big enough to work much, but he did have some chores to do every day. For instance, there were eggs to be gathered, and the cows had to be brought up from pasture at milking time.

One evening when he walked to the pasture, he picked up some stones and threw them, as boys will do today. Among the stones was a "sailer." You know, one of those flat smooth stones, that sails through the air, or skips on the water when you throw it. There were some geese near by, and Walter threw this sailer at them, without thinking that he might hit one of them and injure it.

You can imagine how he felt when he saw that sharp stone hit one of the fine ganders right in the side of the head. The creature whirled around a few times, fell down on the ground, kicked his feet, and then became as still as could be. Walter ran up to him and found that he was dead.

What should he do now? With a troubled conscience he hurried off after the cows, without telling anyone what he had done. When he returned with the cows, he found Grandmother picking the gander in order to save the feathers, and Grandfather stood near, declaring he was going to kill the old turkey gobbler. He had examined the dead gander and concluded that the mark on its head had been made by the turkey gobbler.

Mother and father goose protect their little ones.

Walter stood silently by while Grandpa caught the innocent turkey gobbler, took him to the chopping block, and, with a single stroke of the axe, cut off his head.

When he grew to be a man, Walter said this wrong of his had troubled him thousands of times. In reality he told a lie by remaining silent. He determined then that ever after he would always tell all the facts even if he had to suffer for it. He felt that it would be better to tell the truth, and pay the penalty if necessary, than to keep still and have the innocent suffer for his mistakes.

Walter was quite different from another boy named Harry, who went to work for a very particular man. The boys who had worked for him called him cranky and fussy. It seemed that he had a different boy working for him every week or so, as no one could please him.

Harry doubted if he would be able to satisfy this man Johnson, but his mother felt sure that he could. The wages were good, and the work of opening and closing the shop, sweeping, dusting, and running errands, was not hard work. So Harry decided he would try hard to please this "cranky" man, and if he should fail, he would not be the first one.

Harry had been there only a few days when, one day while sawing some wood, he broke a saw. It frightened him at first. What would Mr. Johnson say? It really was not Harry's fault. He knew how to saw and he had been careful.

One of the boys who had worked for Mr. Johnson came by, and Harry told him what had happened. "You'll get thrashed for that," said the boy.

"It was only an accident," said Harry, "and surely he would expect anyone to have an accident once in a while."

"Accident or no accident," said the boy, "that will make no difference to that old fusser. He had another boy working for him by the name of Leslie. Les was a good boy, too, but one day he accidentally broke some eggs. He didn't dare tell about it. This man Johnson seemed to be suspecting Leslie all the time. Everything that happened about the place Les got blamed for it. He stood it as long as he could, and finally quit."

"Did Leslie tell Mr. Johnson that he broke the eggs?" asked Harry.

"No, of course he didn't tell him. He knew he would lose his temper and fly into a rage."

"I think he should have told him right away," said Harry. "Mr. Johnson might not have been angry."

"I would never tell him. I'd quit first. I know him too well. Do as you like about telling him, but you will find it easier to preach than to practice."

Harry was blue. He felt that he should tell his master about the broken saw, but, after all his boy friend had told him, he felt he might be in for trouble. Mr. Johnson was away, but Harry determined he would break the news to him just the minute he returned. It was late that night when Mr. Johnson came home. Harry had gone to bed. He dressed, and went downstairs to get the disagreeable task off his mind.

"Sir," said Harry, "when I was sawing wood today, I broke your saw, and I thought I should tell you now."

"Weren't you in bed? Why did you get up to tell me about it? Couldn't it wait until morning?"

"Yes, I could have waited, sir, but I felt that if I should put it off till morning, I might be tempted to lie about it. I am sorry I broke it. But I was careful. It was just an accident."

Trembling, Harry waited for a scolding he felt sure would be coming from Mr. Johnson. Instead, the man put his hand on the boy's shoulder, looked at him sympathetically, and said, "Never mind about the broken saw. I am so happy to know that I have a boy now that I can trust. Go to bed and forget all about it."

Imagine how happy Harry was as he climbed the stairs and crawled back into bed! He had been honest, and he slept as only happy boys sleep. He and Mr. Johnson became pals, and Harry found him a true and faithful friend. Harry felt the other boys would have fared better had they been honest.

Chief Kata Ragoso, a Christian teacher of the Solomon Islands, contrasti
the Bible with the idol and weapons his people used to love.

A Doctor's Peculiar Prescription

A LADY who worried and fretted too much about the little things of life, and who was on the verge of a nervous breakdown, came to her physician for help.

She told the doctor how nervous she was, how little things worried her, how things which she had counted as trifles a few years ago now seemed so important and got on her nerves. "I am cross and irritable, Doctor," she said. "I can't be decent to my own family. I say unkind words. I get hysterical. I cry about nothing. My nerves are on edge all the time. What can I do?"

The doctor listened quietly and sympathetically while she told her symptoms, and asked her a few questions. Then, much to her astonishment, he said, "Mrs. Cooper, what you need is to read your Bible more."

The lady was surprised. And it was not difficult for the doctor to see that she felt just a bit hurt. To go to a doctor for physical help and then be told in a roundabout way that there was really nothing wrong with her physically didn't make her feel any too kindly toward him.

Thinking that she had not made herself understood, she made another attempt to tell the doctor her symptoms. He stopped her and said: "Mrs. Cooper, you go home and read your Bible for at least one hour a day for a month. At the end of thirty days come back and see me again. Be sure to follow my advice carefully. I will be glad to see you at the end of the month. Good morning."

Mrs. Cooper was inclined to be a bit upset. At first she thought she would see another doctor, one who might be more understanding and sympathetic. But as she thought about the doctor's advice, she concluded that it was not an expensive prescription anyway. And it was true that she had not opened her Bible in many, many months. She had a copy of the Book some place at home, but it had not been read for a long time. "I'll try his prescription," she said to herself. "It surely won't do me any harm."

So this Christian woman, a church member, went home determined to read the Bible at least an hour a day. She was faithful in following the doctor's orders, and at the end of the month went to see him again.

With a broad smile on his face he welcomed her, saying: "Well, Mrs. Cooper, you have followed my prescription, I see. And you are feeling better, aren't you? You don't want any medicine, do you?"

"No, Doctor," she replied, "I don't need any medicine; I feel like a different person. The world looks different to me. I am much happier, and my family is happier too. I am ashamed that I neglected the Bible as I did."

Turning to his desk the doctor picked up a wellworn Bible. "I read it every day," he said. "If I did not, I would lose my greatest source of strength and skill. It provides help for difficult cases. I never go to an operation without reading something from this Book. I cannot tell you what help it has brought to me, and I felt you did not need medicine, but the peace and comfort which can be found in the Bible."

"To tell you the truth, Doctor, I came very near not taking your prescription," said the lady.

"Many people have refused to take it," he replied. "It is so simple, they have no faith in it."

Strange, isn't it, that a doctor would give such a prescription! But this is a true story, and no doubt many others would profit by it. The Bible does change hearts.

Back on page 96 you will find a photograph of Kata Ragoso, a Solomon Island chief. I saw this man some time ago and heard him tell his story. He has a wonderful face, and is really a wonderful man. We will let him tell what the Bible did for him and the people of the Solomon Islands. While in North America he told his story to millions of people over some of the largest broadcasting stations. He said:

"In the days gone by I did not know, and my fathers before me did not know, of the message of God revealed in His word. Then our works were evil. There was no love in our country. Our customs did not make peace, and we lived in filth. There was always anger, fighting, killing of men, and worshiping of idols. The supposed spirits of our forefathers would take possession of these idols, and, speaking through the devil priests, they would command us to make human sacrifices. Our men and women were always afraid.

"But when the word of God came to us, we were made happy, and our customs were changed. Our villages were made clean. We made good houses. We ate clean food. Our boys and girls went to school, and they have learned to read and write. There are none who have any desire to return to the old customs. We no longer serve idols, or go to distant islands to fight. We no longer kill one another. We no longer take the heads of men to put in the skull houses. We, the children of our forefathers who did these things, no longer do them, for all the old customs have been changed. And the greatest of the things that brought about this change is the Bible."

Many, many years ago, or, to be exact, in the year
1787, King George the Third, of England, fitted out a
small ship called the *Bounty,* manned her with forty-five
sailors and a courageous captain named Bligh, and
started the expedition on a long trip to the South Sea
Islands in the Pacific Ocean.   Some of the islands in the
West Indies, belonging to England, were uninhabited
because there was no food growing on them. So the king
was sending the *Bounty* out to the South Sea Islands, to
gather breadfruit trees, which were to be carried back to
the West Indies and planted there.

Could these brave sailors have known beforehand of
only a few of the adventures they were to meet on this
trip, they might have hesitated to start on such a haz-
ardous journey. The *Bounty* and her crew set sail from
the shores of old England on December 29, 1787, with
provisions on board to last a year and a half.   Just ten
months after they had set sail they arrived at the island
of Tahiti, where they spent six months in gathering the
breadfruit trees, and also in making friends with the
natives of the islands.   Some close friendships were
formed between the sailors and some of the native
women, and when it came time for the *Bounty* to sail,
they found it hard to break away from the friends who
had treated them so kindly during their stay on Tahiti.
In April, 1789, there was evidence of an approaching
storm, and Captain Bligh gave orders for the ship to sail
out to sea.

The *Bounty* had not been at sea very long until the
sailors became very much dissatisfied, and they wished
that they had remained in Tahiti. Captain Bligh was a
hard and tyrannical captain, and as they thought of the
long journey to the West Indies and then the trip home

again, their hearts rebelled, and they determined to turn back to the island and their many friends.

It was a serious offense for sailors to refuse to obey, or to mutiny. In fact, it would mean death, if news of it ever got back to England and they were captured. But realizing all this, on the night of April 28, 1789, four of the men entered Captain Bligh's room, dragged him from his bed, overpowered him, and tied his hands behind him. A small boat was made ready, and the irate captain and eighteen of his men were lowered in the boat to the sea and set adrift. They were given 150 pounds of bread, sixteen pieces of meat averaging two pounds each, six quarts of rum, six bottles of wine, and twenty-eight gallons of water.

It had taken the *Bounty* ten months to make the journey from England, and it seemed almost impossible that they would ever get back home again in just a small row boat. But the strong-hearted captain allotted to each man just so much food and water for each day, and they set out to row 3,600 miles. A few birds were caught now and then for food, and at night they spread their blankets to catch the dew and sucked them in the morning to save water. These resourceful men, encountering every kind of weather, enduring dreadful sufferings, untold hardships, and miseries, finally reached the island of Timor, a Dutch settlement, and were there taken on board a large vessel and were soon safe back in old England.

You are glad, I know, to learn that the captain and his men reached home safely, but what about the *Bounty* and the bold, bad sailors who mutinied? A few of them returned to the island of Tahiti and their friends. But knowing very well that the king of England would not

allow them to go unpunished if they should be captured,
some of them determined to search for some secluded
spot where they might hide themselves and escape punishment.   Their fears were well grounded, for the king
did send out a ship to capture the mutineers, and four-
teen of them were captured.   Ten were returned to England.   Five of these were condemned, and three were
hanged.

Before the king's officers arrived on Tahiti, nine of
the sailors had taken the ship *Bounty,* and with six native men and eleven native women, set sail, searching for
some isolated spot where they might make their home
and be safe from the law.   Fletcher Christian, who now
took command of the *Bounty,* had heard of a small
island in the Pacific named Pitcairn, and they set out
in search of it.   On January 23, 1790, they caught sight
of the island.   When they landed and had explored this
tiny dot of the Pacific, it seemed an ideal place to hide
from the long arm of the British law, for it was only
five miles around the island and but two and a half miles
across it at the widest point, and it was far removed from
the lanes of ocean travel.

Everything they thought they might need was taken
off the *Bounty* to the island, and the ship was then set
afire and burned as an additional safeguard against de-
tection. Imagine how they must have felt—only twenty-
six of them on this little island in the great Pacific, no
homes, no friends, no conveniences, few of life's necessities, and the ship *Bounty*—their only means of leaving
the island—burned.   They set themselves industriously
to building houses and were soon comfortably settled.
The story of the next few years is one of jealousies,
hatreds, treachery, quarrels, and bloodshed.   They

fought and killed one another, until, in the year 1800, John Adams was the sole male survivor of the mutineers —the only man left on the island.

Picture him, if your imagination can, the lone ruler of a godless, helpless, little band of ignorant people. Shut off from the rest of the world on that small island, he had plenty of time to think of his past life and to consider the future of himself and those under his care.

In one of the chests of the sailors, which had been taken from the *Bounty,* he found a book. He read it. It touched his heart and changed his outlook on life. He resolved to live a new life. Can you imagine what book it was? Only one book can make such a change as Adams experienced. It was the Bible. His was a deep and genuine repentance, and he began immediately to teach the women and children the truth of the Bible that had so changed his life. Soon the spirit of all changed, and joy, happiness, and peace reigned in the little island kingdom. Where there had been hatred, there now was love. Their sins and vices were laid aside, and they began to live clean lives. Before this they had been idle and shiftless, but now they began to work and to improve their farms and their homes. A school was started in their midst. They took more pride in their dress and personal appearance. A neat little church was built, and the voice of singing and prayer could often be heard wafting out over the great Pacific. One would hardly believe that they were the same people on the same island. What a wonderful change to be brought about by the reading of a single book!

So great was this change that when, in 1808, the captain of a passing American ship accidentally discovered the inhabitants of Pitcairn and reported them to the

The Pitcairn Islanders beach their boats on the rugged shore.

world, he was able to tell of such a loving, orderly, Christian community that Great Britain, instead of sending a warship to arrest and punish this last survivor of the mutineers, sent gifts of needed supplies and expressions of friendship. To this day the Pitcairn Islanders are a monument to the transforming power of God's word.

What the Bible has done on Pitcairn Island it has done and is still doing in all parts of the world. It will work just as wonderful changes in our towns, in our own lives.

The Bible is a book for young people, for boys and girls. In it they will find stories of heroes and heroines, stories of war, biography, poetry, and even love stories that are true and uplifting. It is the world's most wonderful book.

The noted actress, Ethel Barrymore, picked the Bible as the first textbook for actors. "Not all who read the Bible can act," she said, "but all who act should read the Bible."

Thomas L. Masson, a noted humorist, once said: "I read the Bible two hours a day. The Bible is the best business textbook there is. It makes you cheerful, persistent, honest, and gives you the kind of an understanding that looks through a superficial proposition into the source. It gives you the spiritual power to know how to be provided all the time with the right equipment to carry on your work, and nothing superfluous. Superfluous possessions cause a lot of trouble. Real substance comes from God, and it always comes when needed."

Captain Robert Dollar, who owned the Dollar Steamship Line, or most of the stock in the company, and who died in his eighty-eighth year, read his Bible every day. "By commencing the day with the reading of my

Bible," he said, "I find it gives much valuable information and inspiration which is past my power to express.
The older I become, the more benefit do I derive from the
habit of reading from chapters of the Bible each morning.   It has meant guidance and help in my efforts to
make a success in this world."

There was a Bible in every room of the boats in the
great Dollar fleet, placed there, of course, by Captain
Dollar.

From Rome, sometime ago, the news was cabled that
an Italian of the name of Mercurio Cosma had learned
the whole Bible by heart, and that it had changed his
heart and his life.

This wonderful Book has changed lives, families,
villages, yes, whole countries.   It leaves blessings behind
it always.   Some may not believe it, yet we find that almost every one likes to live where the Bible has gone
before.

A copy of the Bible was given to a Turkish patient
in an American hospital over in Turkey.   When he was
well, he went back to his native village, carrying the
Book with him.   A priest saw the Bible, snatched it
from the Turk, tore it in pieces and threw the fluttering
leaves into the street, and they were carried here and
there by the wind.

A grocer, who happened to be passing, saw some of
the sheets lying on the ground, picked them up, and carried them to his little shop, thinking that they might be
used for wrapping very small parcels.   So as people
came to buy, he used the pages from the Bible for wrap-
pings whenever possible.   He, of course, knew nothing
about the Bible or the messages on the leaves he was
using for wrapping paper.   Soon his customers began to

ask for more leaves. They wanted to know more about the Book. No wonder that when a Bible colporteur called at this little out-of-the-way village, scores of people came hurrying to him, asking for the Bible.

A man on Chicago's South Side, who had lived a wicked life, arose one morning discouraged and sick at heart. He was tired of his ungodly life, and determined that he would end it all. He pulled a revolver from a dresser drawer, planning to shoot himself. But first he decided to turn the radio on, so people in the nearby rooms would not hear the shot. He didn't pick out any particular station, but just turned the dial on at random. A sincere, earnest voice was quoting John 3:16, which says: "For God so loved the world, that He gave His only-begotten Son, that whosoever believeth in Him should not perish, but have everlasting life."

That one verse from the Bible touched his heart. He put the gun away, got down on his knees, and made his peace with God.

Yes, just a verse from the Book has changed a hardened heart. Just a leaf from the Bible has brought hope and courage to those in need.

It is still the world's best seller. And it is the best book in the world—the Book of books.

Bobby and Betty enjoyed farm life.

A Prairie Hailstorm

ON A LARGE farm of 640 acres in sunny Alberta, Canada, lived Mr. and Mrs. Crossland and their two children—Bobby, aged ten; and Betty, aged twelve. They were a happy family.

Mr. Crossland was busy looking after the large farm. He had hired help, of course. Much of the land had to be plowed, and the crops had to be cared for and harvested. Bobby spent many pleasant hours with his father, riding the tractor, following the plow, roaming the fields, romping on the strawstacks, and helping to feed the horses, cows, and chickens. Mother had a real helper in Betty. And there was plenty to do, keeping the house clean and tidy, caring for the milk, washing dishes, and helping to get the meals.

Things hadn't been going any too well for several years. There had been drought, which dried up the land and ruined their wheat crop. Prices had been low, too. So they had gone without many of the things which we often feel are necessary. It meant sacrifice for all of them.

But it was July again. There had been plenty of rain, and their fields were beautiful to look at. The grain was growing rapidly, and they dreamed of the thousands of bushels of wheat which they would be able to sell in the fall. There had been enough rain, and they felt sure that the wheat would mature if it did not rain again that season.

Mrs. Crossland and the children were talking about some of the things they needed and of how they might spend some of the money they expected to get from the crop. All were to have some new clothes. Bob had wanted a bicycle, and if the crop should be good, Mother and Father had promised, he might buy one listed in the catalog. Father had talked of a new car, too. They would all enjoy that. And they might take a trip to see Uncle Jack, who lived several hundred miles way. They got much pleasure out of the planning. A crop seemed so certain that there could be no doubt about it now.

But even as they talked, angry clouds gathered in the west, and before long the rain began to fall. Then it began to hail, and for a few minutes stones almost as large as eggs came pelting against the house. When it stopped, the ground was covered with about two inches of hailstones. They looked out over the wheat fields, and—well—the castles they had built had all tumbled. Their dreams were blighted. Their hearts were sick. The crop had been torn and cut to pieces. There would be no wheat to sell that fall.

The children began to cry, and Mrs. Crossland cried with them. Father came to the house and found the three of them in tears. Then that mother did something really brave and womanly. She dried her tears and tried to comfort the children. Finally she said, "Don't cry children. We have much to be thankful for. You have often wanted ice cream, but we had no ice. Now the yard is covered with ice just the size we need for the freezer. Let's gather up several pails of these hailstones and freeze a big freezer of ice cream."

They were soon busy gathering hailstones and freezing ice cream. They forgot their disappointments, and were happy in spite of them.

Who doesn't have disappointments? Who hasn't

built castles in the air and then has seen them torn down? Who hasn't dreamed dreams which never came true? Who doesn't have troubles now and then? That mother has left us a wonderful example. There will always be disappointments, but they need not discourage us. There are always many things for which we may be thankful. There are always joys within our reach.

A farmer, returning from the field one day, found that an old horse had fallen into an unused cistern. The hole was deep, and the animal had long outlived its usefulness. The man could not devise an easy way to get her out of the well, and he knew that if he did succeed in rescuing her, she wouldn't be any good. The cistern was of no use; in fact, he had threatened to fill it in. What should he do?

The easiest way out was to fill in the cistern and thus bury the old horse. She would be dead in a little while anyway. It was a hard-hearted thing to do, but he got back far enough from the hole so he couldn't see her struggle, and began to shovel in the surrounding earth, hoping old Nell wouldn't suffer long.

But old Nell wasn't ready to die. As the dirt began to fall in on her, she braced her back as best she could. As the earth settled around her, she kept treading it under her feet. The farmer worked feverishly, and the cistern gradually filled in. Old Nell kept on top of the dirt and rose higher and higher until she was able to step out of the cistern and amble off toward the pasture.

Have you ever felt that you were being buried with troubles large and small? If so, you have a great deal of company. Every one has his trials and burdens, and many of us feel that our load is a little heavier than anyone else's.

I wonder, if we could all dump our troubles in one large heap, and then go to the pile of tribulation and pick the trial or affliction or trouble we would prefer, whether most of us wouldn't scratch around in the pile until we should find the same old burden again.

Some of us make trouble for ourselves, and some of us think too much about our trials and afflictions. We nurse them; we coddle them and advertise them. It is possible to be buried by them, or to use them, as did the old horse—to lift us to greater heights.

WHAT GREAT GRANDMOTHER SAID TO ME

Once on a time, as I sat on her knee,
My greatgrandmother sang to me,
"If all our troubles were hung on a line,
You would take yours and I would take mine."
Since then full many and many a time
Have I thought of that simple, little rhyme
When I felt my worries and troubles and care
Were more than other folks had to bear.
And I said to myself, "If it could be—
This song I learned at my grandmother's knee!
But I know my cares must be greater far
Than those of complaining neighbors are."
But now, with the years that have passed, I see
The truth of what Grandmother sang to me—
"If all our troubles were hung on a line,
You would take yours and I would take mine."
                              —*Florence Jones Hadley,*
                              in "New Outlook."

Prayer for a School

OVER the entrance of the first building erected at Bethune-Cookman College at Daytona Beach, are the words "Faith Hall." The inscription is but the brief story of a struggle on the part of Mary McLeod Bethune to secure school privileges for colored youth in the South.

With exactly $1.65 on hand, and a borrowed, four-room cottage, she began her school. In her first class there were only five little girls and one boy—her own son.

She had no supplies with which to carry on her work. There just were none. "We burned logs," she explains, "and used the charred splinters as pencils, and mashed elderberries for ink. I begged strangers for a broom, a lamp, a bit of cretonne to put around the packing case which served as my desk. I haunted the city dump and the trash piles behind hotels, picking up cracked dishes, broken chairs, discarded linen, pieces of old lumber. Everything was scoured and mended. This was part of the training—to salvage, to reconstruct, to make bricks without straw. As parents began to leave their children overnight, I had to provide beds. I took corn sacks for mattresses. Then I picked Spanish moss from trees, dried and cured it, and used it as a substitute for mattress hair."

Often there was nothing with which to carry on. After working and begging she still had times when food was not on hand for students. On one such occasion she tried to get one dollar's worth of supplies. But the grocer would not listen. He must have cash, and

Mrs. Mary McLeod Bethune's faith helped her to start her famous sch

cash only, for his food. He could not see through Mrs. Bethune's small project, worthy though it was.

On her way home she was very discouraged. How could she explain to the children? How could she keep her school going? As she walked along the road home she prayed, laying her case before Him who watches over the young and unwary.

Then something unusual happened. She looked up when she neared home, and there on the porch were four of her adult pupils. They were waiting to see her to pay a dollar each for classes they had attended weeks before. Mrs. Bethune was very happy. The Lord had heard her prayer and had sent through these people exactly enough funds to get the groceries needed. The men were surprised to hear her thank God for the money they gave. They were invited to go with her and bring home the purchases.

At one time she was preparing for a large dinner for the pupils at Christmas time. Everything was in readiness, and then the dishes were called in by a woman who had loaned them to the school. Some of the children began to cry, but Mrs. Bethune said, "Be quiet, the Lord will provide."

Then a butler from one of the resort homes stumbled in the door with a large basket. "Mrs. Lawrence Thompson," he said, "sent this basket of dishes; her son just gave her a beautiful new set as a Christmas present."

Students came to school in larger numbers. New needs were met by prayer and faith. She bought a very poor lot of ground for $200, with an agreement to pay five dollars down and five dollars every month that she could find it. "He never knew it," adds Mrs. Bethune, "but at the time I didn't even have the first five dollars. But I got it all right—by selling ice cream and sweet potato pies to workmen who were putting up some new buildings at the beach.

Thus began a great school from a persevering effort.

And so it is no wonder that she named the first building "Faith Hall." It speaks of the way God helped in the education of boys and girls who otherwise might have followed a very unprofitable life course.

Drive On!

A MANUFACTURER of brooms in Ohio, in an earlier day, shipped his product across the country in the old prairie schooner or covered wagon. At one time he ordered a load of brooms sent to Pittsburgh, Pennsylvania, which was about sixty miles distant. The teamster was new at the business; in fact, it was his first trip.

He managed to get along very well with his load until he reached the west bank of the Alleghany River, which was no small stream at that season of the year. It was crossed by one of the old-fashioned covered bridges. When he approached the entrance to the long wooden bridge, he stopped his team and viewed the structure with quite a bit of concern and indecision. After some moments of perplexed thought, he turned around and drove back home—almost sixty miles.

Of course, his employer wondered what could have happened to bring the man back with his load of brooms undelivered. The driver explained that when he reached the covered bridge, he looked through to the far end, and since the opening on the opposite side of the river was so very small, he decided that he could never get through it with his load of brooms. Therefore, he had returned. Of course, he did not do any more driving for that business man. He lost his job for lack of vision. He did not have that quality which all successful men and women must have—that quality of going on, even when one cannot see his way through. In other words, he lacked *perseverance*.

117

The old covered bridges are disappearing; in fact, most of them are gone. But there are still many thousands, yes, millions of persons who start for "Pittsburgh," but do not reach their destination, and fall short of the goal they set for themselves. Why? Because, when things look dark, and they cannot see daylight ahead, they give up and turn back.

Thomas Alva Edison, when experimenting with his phonograph, could not see his way through. It just would not say the letter "s." But he drove on. Sixteen hours a day, and six days a week for six months, he persevered until success came. And after many honors had come to him, he was humble enough to say that what he had been able to accomplish was more the result of perspiration than of inspiration.

Disraeli, as a young man, decided that he was one day going to be prime minister of England. His way was often blocked, but he went either through or around every difficulty. His first speech in Parliament was a joke to many of his fellow members, and they hissed him to his seat. His remark in answer to their jibes and hisses shows the mettle of the man. He said: "The time will come when you will hear me."

He drove on toward the premiership, and reached his goal.

For six years Adoniram Judson preached to the Buddhists of Burma before he knew of a single convert. Time after time he and his faithful wife celebrated the ordinances alone. At the conclusion of the Lord's supper, they would say, "We are the church of Jesus in Burma."

When Judson had been in the field five years, some one wrote to him and asked what the prospects were for the conversion of the heathen. "As bright as the promises of God," he replied. This faithful couple persevered until a foundation was laid and souls were won.

The battles of the world have been won by going on —and on—and on! For twenty years James Whitcomb Riley tried to sell his poems, but without success. He drove on.

Clarence Budington Kelland received sixty-four rejection slips before his first story was sold.

Pasteur, wearied by thousands of experiments, all of which seemed to have been time and money wasted, was almost discouraged; but before the light of hope flickered and went out entirely, he tried "one more" experiment, and it gave us some wonderful discoveries concerning disease germs. How much his "going on" has meant to mankind!

Early in youth Abraham Lincoln decided to give his life to his country, but for a long, long time, it seemed to him that the nation did not want his services. He ran for the Legislature and was defeated; he tried to get into Congress and failed; he sought a position in the General Land Office, and was turned down. Twice he was defeated as candidate for the United States Senate. He lost out in his first effort to be nominated for the presidency, but at last gained the greatest gift in the hands of the American people, and became their best-loved President. Then came the greatest test of his life—the Civil War. When criticisms fell like rain, when battles were being lost daily, when failure seemed certain and imminent, when trusted men turned traitor, and when generals surrendered, he remained firm in the dogged determination to go on to victory. And his "going on" preserved the Union.

Some one asked Stradivarius, "How long does it take to make a violin?"

He answered, "A thousand years."

Then he went on to explain that "violins made from young trees, shielded from the storm, could never be fashioned into masterpieces. It requires 1,000 years in

Careful persistence is important for the scientist in his laboratory.

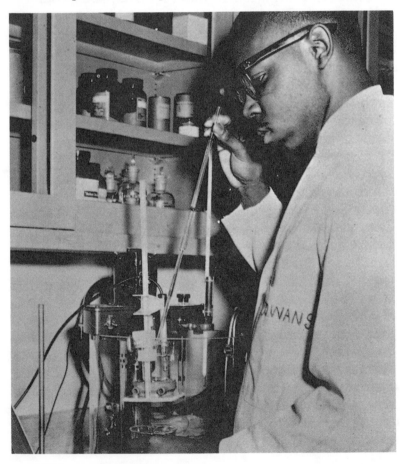

which the tree is tempered by tempest, tried by wind, beaten by sleet and hail, covered by snow, drenched by rain, scorched by the summer's blighting breezes, and blasted by the icy breath of winter. A thousand years are necessary in which to strengthen and exercise the arms of the branches by the gnarling of the tempests— to rejoice with fair lovers under its cooling shade—to weep with mother birds at the destruction of the young —to whistle with the gentle zephyrs of night rustling in its leaves in moonlight sonatas of love and hope." But from this time of testing would come timber which, when properly seasoned and fashioned, might be made into a real violin.

Friends of Stradivarius made sport of him because he spent so much time and took so much pains in making his instruments. Today he ranks with the great and the good, while those who criticized him sank into oblivion at their death.

In northern California was a deserted mine shaft which, years before, had been worked by a lone prospector. For long months, during the gold rush, he had labored in his search for gold. With pick and shovel, drill and dynamite, he had blasted and picked his way through rock, limestone, and earth, toward the heart of the mountain, hoping always that he might be rewarded with the precious yellow metal. Long months of arduous labor brought no encouragement, no rewards. Discouragement overcame him. He left his picks, shovels, dynamite, all his equipment, and went away from the mine, never to go back. He was satisfied that there was no use in his going on.

Years later a large mining company found the shaft, and their engineers advised them to buy the property

and reopen the deserted mine. They cleared out the
fallen rocks, earth, and debris, and were soon at the place
where the discouraged prospector had left his tools and
quit.

With modern equipment, the new company began
operations. Six inches farther on they struck a rich
vein of gold. Only six inches of rock separated the
young prospector from success and his heart's desire.
Had he gone on only six inches more, his life's dreams
would have come true. Only six inches more!

Many of you who read these lines may feel as the
young prospector felt—that there is no use in trying to
go on. Maybe you have spent long years in preparation
for your life work, and now that you have your education, find no opening, no place in which to use your tal-
ents. Perhaps you have set a goal for yourself and have
been struggling and working to reach it, yet find yourself a long, long way from your destination. Perchance
you have been overcome by temptations, have stumbled,
and have fallen.

The battles of successful men and women have
been won by going on. "Life's struggles against storms
within and tempests without have been won by going
on."

Young friends, don't lay down your tools. Work,
fight on, until the conquest ends in victory, and you have
reached your goal. There may be rich veins of gold
only "six inches farther on." Perhaps you can't just
see your way through. The opening in the "old covered
bridge" may appear too small. There is nothing to be
gained by going back; so why not "drive on"?

Skyscraper or Shanty

IN MOST of our cities today there are restricted areas, where only a certain type of house may be built. When you buy a lot in one of these districts, you buy with the understanding that you must spend a certain amount, say $10,000 or more, in the erection of a building. No shacks, no, not even a modest bungalow will be permitted.

To each of us has been allotted a little space in this old world—a lot, if you please to call it such. And on it we are building—building characters. There are no restricted areas, however; we may build either a skyscraper or a shanty. We decide what the structure will be.

Those of you who are young are putting in the foundation to the building. Some are putting on the finishing touches. If I could see what sort of foundation you are putting in today, in the days of your youth, I could predict quite accurately just what your building will be—hovel or palace.

Every normal, ambitious young man and woman wants to build large. No one will admit that he is planning on putting up a shanty on the shifting sands of time.

How often I have seen great holes being dug on vacant lots in the heart of a great city—getting ready for a foundation. Day after day the groaning, hissing steam shovel dug out the earth and loaded it into trucks and wagons until the digging got right down to bed rock. And when I saw them going down, down, down, I knew

A tall building, like a person's life, would soon collapse without a strong foundation.

full well there would be a building going up, up, up into the clouds.

I have seen carpenters, too, laying timbers on a few cement or wooden blocks, getting ready for a building. Without asking questions, I knew they were planning to build a garage or a chicken house, or some mere shanty. Youth is the foundation time of life. On the foundation you build today must rest the superstructure of to-morrow. The habits you are forming while young are the stones in this foundation. One unsound, defective stone may weaken the whole structure.

A few years ago I was privileged to work with a very talented man. He had a good education, a pleasing personality, a keen intellect. I envied his abilities. I wondered for a time why a man of such rare ability had not climbed higher and filled positions of more responsibility. But I had not worked with him long until I knew just why. He had worked into the foundation of his character a stone we might call sarcasm. He could pack more biting, stinging sarcasm into a letter than any man I ever knew. He could say in a few words the most cruel things. He seemed to delight in those cutting humiliating jibes, whether by letter or word of mouth. That stone in his character marred his building and kept him from greater responsibilities.

In college I had a classmate who was brilliant, talented, good-natured, and well liked by his fellow students. He was cultured and courteous. He dressed neatly, and always appeared well. But he had a pet weakness. He was tardy to his classes, late to his meals —in fact, never on time for anything. If he has not overcome that weakness, he will never succeed in life.

A short time ago I visited a large penitentiary.

They were enlarging the institution, and the inmates
were doing the work. About fifty men, all clad in blue
denim uniforms, each with a number on his back, were
building a huge stone wall. Nearby were a number of
khaki-clad guards, each equipped with a high-powered
rifle. They were watching every move made by the men
in blue. Stone by stone they built the wall—a wall
that, later on, would imprison them,—keep them from
freedom and liberty. As I watched them I thought,
"How like us are these men, for we are day by day
forming habits, which if they be the wrong kind, imprison us, make slaves of us, keep us from success in
life."

A few weeks ago I boarded a night train in Toronto,
Canada, starting on a 3,000-mile journey to the Northwest. I had just gotten into bed when a drunken man
entered and took the berth near me. He was so intoxicat-
ed that he had difficulty in getting into bed. The next
morning he slept until almost eleven o'clock. I wish I
might describe to you just how he looked when he
crawled from his berth. He was a man past sixty, his
countenance telling plainly of his life of dissipation.
There was a rum blossom on the end of his nose. He did
not need to tell any one that he felt miserable.

His system was calling for more drink, but we were
many miles from any place where it could be bought.
In his desperation he drank liquid soap from the container in the men's washroom. An hour or so brought
us to a division point, and he was off to buy more liquor.
He came back in a few minutes well supplied, and before long he was happy again—drunk as could be. He
drank more or less through the afternoon, and at night
he staggered from the train, drunk—a slave to a habit

formed earlier in life. Many young men and women are today starting out full of ambition and hope, yearning for worlds to conquer, but like Alexander of old they have not gotten the victory over their own vices, their appetites, and they fail. How sad it is to see a young person virtually chained to a habit—a slave.

I was out on the Atlantic not long ago, headed toward home. Our boat was to dock that morning, and I got up early to see the sights. Another passenger had gotten out before I had, and he was nervously pacing the deck when he noticed me. A ray of hope seemed to flit across his troubled countenance as he came my way. "Say, friend," he said, almost pleadingly, "have you got a match? I just have to have a smoke, and I can't find a match any place."

I was sorry to tell him that I did not, for although I don't smoke, and really loathe the weed and its smell, I felt sorry for him. He was miserable. He was a slave, and his master was lashing him furiously.

Some years ago an edict went forth that the cotton acreage was to be reduced. To comply with this government order, it was necessary in certain sections of the South to plow up every other row of cotton in the great fields. This reduction of crop, it was felt, would help revive the cotton market. The farmers of the South took their mules and went into the fields to plow up the cotton. But they met with a real difficulty. For years their mules had been taught to walk between the rows of cotton, and in order to plow them up they had to make the animals walk down the row itself. The mules refused. For every well-trained mule, each row of cotton might as well have carried a sign, "Don't Tread on Me." They just wouldn't "stomp" down the cotton.

They were only mules, but their owners found it difficult to get them to break a habit formed through the years.

Did you ever hear of any one's building a skyscraper, and when it was all finished, putting in the foundation? No, you have not, for it is too foolish to even think about. It cannot be done. It is impossible. It is just as impossible to neglect one's character building when young, and expect to build a life and slip in a foundation in later years. It just isn't done. Neither do they build skyscrapers on a few cement blocks or wooden supports laid on top of the ground. If you are planning on a skyscraper, put in a skyscraper foundation on bed rock. If you are going to build just a shanty, any old foundation will do. But you must decide now. When you get to manhood and womanhood it will be rather late to work on the foundation.

"Our wrong habits cannot be taken to heaven with us, and unless overcome here, they will shut us out of the abode of the righteous," says a godly writer.

For twenty years a great towering mass of rock three hundred feet high formed a peak overlooking Thormery, France. Daily it was being undermined by the weather, and the residents of Thormery were in constant fear that it might fall and bury them. They bored holes in its base and blew it up with dynamite.

Have you some habit threatening the ruin of your character? Don't compromise with it. Blow it to pieces.

A Great Benefactor

MANY of the world's greatest men and women began life under the most forbidding circumstances. Of humble birth, and with few advantages, they have traveled a rugged path to success and usefulness, while others more favored enjoyed only a mediocre life. We like to read of the section man who became president of the railroad, or of the journey of some ambitious youth from log cabin to fame and fortune.

One of the most inspiring biographies of the past century is that of Booker T. Washington. Although he has laid down his burdens and passed on to his rest, his life will ever be an encouragement to struggling young men and women.

His life began in the most wretched, miserable, and disheartening surroundings. The little, one-roomed log cabin in which he was born had no floor except the earth, no glass windows, and a door that was one only in name. There were wide cracks in the sides of the building, and the openings made for windows let in more cold than light. In this humble cabin lived Booker, his older brother John, his sister Amanda, and his mother, who was the plantation cook. About his father he knew nothing. The mother was busy from early morning until late at night, and the children received little attention from her. For a bed they had a pile of rags on the dirt floor. Their food was meager.

School for Booker was not thought of. He remembers going as far as the schoolhouse door to carry books

Booker T. Washington helped many to live better lives.

for one of the plantation girls, but he never got inside the door, although in his little heart he longed to go. His first pair of shoes were of wood. One of his most trying ordeals as a boy was to break in a new flax shirt. It was a painful experience, but it was either to wear the shirt and endure the torture or to go without anything on, for this one garment was all that he had to wear.

The Civil War came, and at its close came the freedom of the slaves. Booker's stepfather, immediately after the Emancipation Proclamation, found work in a West Virginia salt furnace, and decided to move his family thither. It was a long, eventful trip over the mountains, the simple household effects being packed into a cart, and the children walking most of the distance, which was several hundred miles.

Settling in Malden, the stepfather soon began work in the salt furnace, and Booker was taken along, though only a boy, to help earn a living. They began work as early as four in the morning. It was here at his work that the little fellow gathered his first book knowledge, and this bit of learning was as a tiny seed planted in his heart, which began to grow forthwith, and could not be choked out by the most discouraging circumstances nor the gloomiest outlook.

His stepfather's number in the salt works was eighteen, and at the close of the day the foreman of the packers would come and put on each barrel they had filled the figure 18. Booker soon learned this figure, and also how to make it. This was the beginning of his education. He determined then and there, if he should accomplish nothing else in life, he would get enough education to read books and papers. He told his mother of his aspirations, and sharing his ambitions, she managed in some way to secure for him a copy of Webster's old "blue-back" spelling book, which he began at once to devour.

About this time he got added inspiration from a boy who came to Malden. This young fellow had learned to read, and at the close of the day's work the crowds would gather around him, and he would read aloud to them from the newspaper. Booker envied this young hero, and his attainments seemed to be the acme of accomplishment.

Booker implored, entreated, begged his parents to permit him to go to school, but he had a commercial value to the father, who therefore hesitated to give his consent. It was finally arranged that the boy might go to school provided he would arise at four in the morning and work in the salt furnace until nine, and then return to work again after school. To this Booker willingly agreed.

Other difficulties presented themselves. Up to this time in his experience he had never worn anything on his head, but he found on going to school that all the other boys had hats or caps. He had no money with which to buy a cap, so his mother helped him over this difficulty by making a cap for him out of two pieces of "homespun."

The next problem which confronted him was in regard to his name. The first morning in school the teacher began to call the roll, and Booker noticed that all the other boys and girls had two names, and some of them even three. He had never had any other name than Booker, and was perplexed, of course. By the time the teacher reached him, he had solved the problem and responded, "Booker Washington," a name which followed him until his death.

Circumstances compelled him to stop school, and he found work in a mine with his stepfather. One day, in the darkness of the mine, he heard a conversation between two workmen, and this influenced his after life. From this dialogue he learned of a school for colored people who were too poor to pay money for their education. The young people could work to pay for their schooling. At that time he did not find out just where the school was, nor how many miles away it might be, nor how to reach it, but then and there he determined he would go to Hampton, and this ambition he kept constantly in mind. He told his mother of his cherished plans, and she encouraged him in his dreams.

By walking and begging rides, he reached Richmond, Virginia, tired and exhausted from his long journey. Finding no lodging, he spent the night under a slight elevation in a boardwalk. In the morning he found work helping to unload a cargo of pig iron. He worked there for several days, going back each night to his bed beneath the sidewalk. Many years after, the citizens of Richmond tendered him a public reception not far from this same spot.

In his autobiography he says that the first glimpse he got of the school at Hampton paid him for all the sacrifices he had made to get there. He did not appear to be the most promising student when he presented himself for entrance to the school, for he had been on the journey a long time and was nearly exhausted.

His entrance examination was the sweeping of a classroom in the college. One of the teachers handed him a broom and said, "The adjoining recitation

Today's boys and girls will be the important people of tomorrow.

room needs sweeping. Take the broom and sweep it."
Realizing that much depended upon this simple test,
he swept the room three times and then dusted it four
times, not missing a nook or corner. When he had
finished, the teacher came to inspect his work and taking
her white handkerchief, she rubbed it over the table and
some of the woodwork. Not finding one particle of
dust or dirt, she quietly remarked, "I guess you will do
to enter this institution."

To him these were the sweetest words his ears had
ever heard. He had passed his "entrance examination," and he was one of the happiest souls on earth.

There were many things to learn. "Life at Hampton," says Mr. Washington in his autobiography, "was
a constant revelation to me; was constantly taking me
into a new world. The matter of having meals at reg-
ular hours, of eating on a table cloth, using a napkin,
and the use of the bathtub and the toothbrush, as well
as the use of sheets upon the bed, were all new to me."

When he went to Hampton, he had never slept in
a bed or between two sheets. So the sheets were a puzzle
to him. The first night he slept under both sheets, and
the second night on top of them, but by watching the
other boys he learned how to sleep between them.

When you think of the fact that he arrived at
Hampton with only fifty cents in his pocket, and that
he finished the course offered there, working his way,
your imagination will picture some of the struggles
this young man had, so we need not mention them in de-
tail.

Finishing the course of study at Hampton, he returned to his former home in Malden, and was elected
to teach the school. "This," he says, "was the begin-

ning of one of the happiest periods of my life. I felt now I had the opportunity to help the people of my home town to a higher life."

The only true happiness any of us enjoy in this life comes from having been a blessing to some one else. Working from early morning until late at night, he endeavored to teach the boys and girls, not only to read and write, but to wash their hands and comb their hair, to use the toothbrush, and to follow other hygienic measures.

That he might do more for his community and for the people of the South generally, he started a school at Tuskegee, in 1881, and patterned it after the school at Hampton. While young people here were given an education from books, they were taught much more. They learned the dignity of labor. They got their "first taste of what it meant to live a life of unselfishness," and learned that "the happiest individuals are those who do the most to make others useful and happy."

At Hampton Mr. Washington had learned a lesson which he sought to impart to all his students, one which every young person should learn: that "it is not a disgrace to labor; that we should love labor, not for its financial value alone, but for labor's own sake and for the independence and self-reliance which the ability to do something which the world wants done, brings." The young man or woman who has learned this lesson has an advantage over him who has not realized this.

The life of Booker T. Washington shows the power of a dominant purpose. His life of struggle should be an encouragement to struggling young men and women. His ambitions and attainments should inspire to higher ideals and to loftier accomplishments.

Head Winds and Tail Winds

I ONCE traveled by automobile from Ontario to California. Every day we pushed against a strong west wind. Time and time again as we journeyed, I wished that the wind might let up a bit, or better still, that it might swing around to the east, and give us a little help instead of resisting us hour after hour and mile after mile. But it did not change; day after day we drove against the wind. We made good time, in spite of the opposition; the engine kept cool and functioned perfectly. We patiently endured that west wind, consoling ourselves that when we returned, it would be at our back.

And sure enough, on the return journey, it was as we had hoped. The first day or two of the trip we drove through the desert, and the sun was on duty early and late. The engine kept getting hotter and hotter. It had not heated up before, and I felt something must be wrong, so made sure there was enough oil and plenty of water. But still it got hot. So I drove into a garage and asked for some advice. "It's that tail wind, mister," the mechanic assured me. "Those tail winds are bad. If you were going against the wind you would have no trouble."

How like life! Some of us have to face strong head winds every day of our lives. Life seems to be just one long struggle. Others seem to have the advantage of a tail wind—no struggles, no problems, no troubles, some one to help them along. From earliest childhood they are coddled and protected by fond parents. They get

Tail winds can push huge jets along even faster.

so into the habit of being pushed along that they cannot face even an opposing breeze.

The chicken which is helped out of the shell seldom lives when he gets out in the big cold world. The oak tree protected from storms does not send its roots far into the earth.

Do you ever get to feeling sorry for yourself when you have been facing head winds day after day and month after month until they run into years? Have you ever wished you might have been born rich so as to avoid the struggles of poverty? Do you have some physical handicap which to you often seems too heavy a burden to bear? Have your plans failed, your air castles tumbled, your dreams failed to come true?

Let us look into the lives of a few of our fellow men.

Are you poor? Poverty need not be a handicap. This continent of ours was discovered by a man who had to beg for money and ships to make the voyage across an unknown sea.

Lincoln didn't have money to buy books, and did some of his homework in arithmetic with pieces of charcoal on a wooden shovel before the flickering light of the fireplace.

Shakespeare held horses at the door of a London theater. Robert Burns began life as a plowboy on the farm. Martin Luther was the son of a poor miner, and sang from door to door, begging for his daily food.

The great evangelist, Gypsy Smith, was born in a gypsy wagon. When he was taken to London and invited to the home of a friend who was interested in the boy, he met many difficulties. He had never slept in a bed, so wondered just how to get into it. His napkin at the table he used for a handkerchief.

Hudson Maxim, the great inventor, had neither a hat nor a pair of shoes until he was thirteen years of age. He walked two miles to school barefooted, even when there was snow on the ground.

Dwight L. Moody was left fatherless when only four years old. There were nine children in the family and the stony farm on which they lived was heavily mortgaged. The creditors took everything—even the wood from the woodpile. During his childhood Dwight was "knocked about from pillar to post."

Carey, the father of modern missions, was a humble shoe cobbler.

Peter, the great apostle, was a humble fisherman, and Jesus our Saviour had no place to lay His head.

F. W. Woolworth, founder of the five-and-ten-cent stores, faced the head wind of poverty. He was so poor that he went barefooted six months in the year, and had no overcoat in the winter. Feeling sure the old farm near Watertown, New York, promised no future for him, he determined to go into business. He hitched up the old horse and drove into Carthage, New York. Here he went from store to store applying for work. The merchants of Carthage didn't know what was wrapped up in that awkward, gawky, country lad. So he got no encouragement.

Finally, however, a man who was operating a store as a sort of sideline let Woolworth work for him just for the experience.

Later he got work in a dry-goods store. Here he did the janitor work, ran errands, and waited on a few customers during rush hours. The owner of this store wanted him to work for nothing for six months, but young Woolworth had only fifty dollars, money he had saved while on the farm, so he couldn't work long without pay. It was finally agreed that he should work three months without any remuneration, and then he would receive fifty cents a day for fifteen hours' work.

He found work in another store at ten dollars a week, but he did not stay long. The employer reminded him daily that he was no good, cut his wages, and threatened to discharge him.

His nerves couldn't stand up under the strain. He had to return to the farm, and for a twelve-month period could not work at all. He must have complete rest. He was so disheartened that he was about to abandon the idea of business, when one cold, blustery day in March he received a message from one of his former employers. He wanted him to come to work. Frank's father was taking some potatoes to market that day, so the boy crawled up on the load and rode into town with him.

Somehow he got the idea of opening some stores where nothing would cost more than five cents, and borrowed three hundred dollars to start the venture. Some of his stores failed, but he was careful and cautious. Today his red-front stores may be found in all of our cities. He became one of the wealthiest men in America. He faced head winds most of his life.

Will Rogers became one of the most loved men in America, a great humorist who never made fun of any man's religion or his nationality. He said that he never met a man he didn't like. The first time he went to New York, he traveled on a freight train with a load of cattle all the way from Oklahoma. People made fun of him as he traveled about New York in his cowboy clothes. But he made a name for himself, and in later years he flew to New York, and instead of jeering at him, people were courting his favor and begging for his autograph. He faced head winds, plenty of them.

Benjamin Franklin began life in humble surroundings as the son of a tallow-candle maker. He later became a journeyman printer, and fought his way to success. Charles Dickens was a label sticker in a shoe-blacking factory. John Wanamaker began life at $1.25 a week. S. J. Hungerford, president of the Canadian National Railways, one of the largest railroad systems in the world, began as a day laborer on the road—wages $4.50 a week.

Lowell Thomas, one of the best known news reporters in North America, got his start selling newspapers in Cripple Creek, Colorado, a very rough gold mining district. To get an education he fired furnaces, carried out ashes, worked in restaurants, sold real estate, acted as tutor, in fact did anything he could get to do. He worked hard and kept himself clean. He does not smoke, drink, or gamble, and is one of America's foremost radio commentators.

The songs "I Love You Truly" and "Just a Wearyin' for You" were written by Carrie Jacobs Bond on scraps of wrapping paper by candlelight. She was too poor to buy writing paper, and the candlelight was much cheaper than gas.

She was happily married to a young doctor. Their wedded life was short for, one night, when calling on a patient in the woods of northern Michigan, he fell on the ice, and died an agonizing death. She was left to face the world with a young son and a load of debts.

She moved to Chicago and tried running a rooming house. This venture was a failure. Then she tried painting china and writing songs. Hand-painted china was a luxury, and publishers returned the songs she wrote.

Her furniture was sold to pay the rent, and she went to bed to keep warm when her daily allowance of fuel had been used. She was so poor at one time that she could afford only one meal a day.

She had no money to advertise her songs, and did sewing for a lady editor to pay for advertising space. She tried singing her songs. The first time she attempted this she was hissed off the stage, and fled, heartbroken, from a rear exit of the building.

At one time she was asked to sing before the governor of Illinois, but had nothing fit to wear. She must keep this appointment, so pulled some old lace curtains and some remnants from a trunk, and from these made a gown for the occasion.

One evening, after a pleasant journey with friends amid the beauties of the Pacific Coast, she wrote the poem "The End of a Perfect Day," and found herself humming a tune to accompany it. Her financial worries were over. More than 6,000,000 copies of this song were sold, and the profits to her were perhaps $250,000. She had the joy and satisfaction of knowing that her songs were proving a blessing to millions. She was asked to sing at the White House, by President Theodore Roosevelt, and later by President Harding. She even went across the ocean to sing her songs.

Robert Ripley was fired from the first three newspaper jobs at which he worked. His father, a carpenter, wanted Bob to be a bricklayer or a plumber, and tried to discourage the boy from being an artist. But the boy was not easily discouraged.

Thomas Alva Edison was a puny, sickly child, and

there was only one person who had faith to believe he would ever amount to anything. Doctors said his head was very odd shaped and that he would have some kind of brain trouble. His teacher in the primary school that he attended in Ohio told "Al" that he was "addled," and that it was a shame for his parents to waste their money in trying to teach him anything. He spent only three months in school. His mother had been a teacher, and she had confidence in the boy. So she took him out of school and taught him herself. When eleven years old, he became interested in chemistry, but had no money to carry on his experiments. To earn some money he sold papers on the train that ran between Detroit and Port Huron. A hot-headed conductor on this run one day slapped Edison's ears and left him almost deaf for the rest of his life. He was not discouraged by sickness, dullness, or deafness. He plodded on to success. When offered $100,000 for his first invention, he felt it must be a dream. Just a short time before this he had arrived in New York, not only penniless, but in debt. He roamed the streets hungry and without funds. Thus the world's greatest inventor began life with more handicaps than most of us have known. But he refused to give up. He read good books, worked, and made use of his spare time.

John Bunyan wrote *Pilgrim's Progress* while confined in Bedford jail. This book has had a larger circulation than any other book, except the Bible. John the apostle wrote the book of Revelation while in exile on the Isle of Patmos.

Do you have physical handicaps? If so, do not allow them to discourage you. Fannie Crosby, when an infant in her mother's arms, was left blind through the blunders of an ignorant country doctor. She must go through life in total darkness. A poem which she wrote when only eight years old should be an encouragement to any boy or girl who may have physical handicaps to fight. She said:

"Oh what a happy soul am I!
Although I cannot see,
I am resolved that in this world
Contented I will be.

"How many blessings I enjoy,
That other people don't,
To weep and sigh because I'm blind,
I cannot and I won't."

Though confined to her room through the long years of her life by blindness, she wrote more than 8,000 hymns, and they have been sung in all parts of the civilized world. From behind that wall of darkness came streams of light which shall never grow dim—which have brought courage and joy into countless lives.

Her cheerful, optimistic outlook on life, and' her simple childlike faith in God can be seen in all her writings, and should be an encouragement to any who are struggling with physical handicaps. If something went wrong, she always reasoned that "it might have been worse." "I have long since learned," she said, "that 'what can't be cured, must be endured.' Some days are good, some days are ill. But it never pays to murmur, and it is useless to worry."

As she sat alone, thinking of her blindness, she said to herself, "Fanny, there are many worse things than blindness that might have happened to you. The loss of the mind is a thousand times worse than the loss of the eyes. Then I might have been speechless and deaf. I do not know but that on the whole it has been a good thing that I have been blind. How in the world could I have lived such a helpful life as I have lived had I not been blind? I never let anything trouble me, and to my simple faith, and to my implicit trust in my heavenly Father's goodness, I attribute my good health and long life. In the case of my loss of sight I can see how the Lord permitted it. He didn't order it; He permitted it."

By her hymns, as well as by her life, she preached faith, hope and courage to millions.

Napoleon Bonaparte was an epileptic, but in spite of this malady became a great military genius. Robert Louis Stevenson was a victim of tuberculosis and wrote many of his child rhymes while propped up in his bed.

Helen Keller was blind and deaf. Michelangelo, the great artist and sculpter, was a chronic sufferer from fever. Milton the great writer, was blind.

Elizabeth Barrett Browning, the Shakespeare of English women, suffered a nervous breakdown at the age of thirteen, and from that day on was a constant sufferer. Years of her life were spent in a darkened room alone.

Einstein as a child was subnormal. His teachers were bored by him. He was backward, shy, dull, and extremely slow. No one thought he would ever amount to anything.

Richard Byrd was retired from the United States Navy at the age of twenty-eight as physically unfit for service. He had broken a foot and was so lame the government couldn't use him. He said that he could fly a plane sitting down, and so he became an aviator. He wanted to fly over the frozen areas of the North, and planned to fly in the *Shenandoah,* the huge dirigible which crashed on its test flight. He tried to get the government to let him make some test flights with the goal of crossing the Atlantic in mind. But they refused. Amundsen planned a trip across the Arctic wastes, and Byrd begged for permission to fly one of the planes in this expedition, but again the government refused. These were disappointments, but not discouragements. He secured funds from private parties to finance his expeditions. He flew the Atlantic, flew to the North Pole, and then to the South pole. When he returned, the government that had turned him out of the navy and refused his services as an aviator, made him an admiral, and the world received him with open arms.

Mary Roberts Rinehart did much of her writing in beds and wheel chairs. She has often remarked that she would never have written so many books had it not been for a siege of operations and so much illness. Harrassed by debts, she began her writing when the mother of three babies. She wanted to do all she could to help her physician husband, who had lost his savings in a stock-market crash. She was busy with her housework in the daytime and up much at night with the babies. But in spite of her many duties, many evenings, when dead tired from the day's toil, she spent her time writing. She once wrote a book of poems for children and attempted to find a market for it in New York City. She trudged the streets, going from one publisher to another, in a vain attempt to sell her manuscript.

For the first manuscript she sold she received thirty-four dollars. She wrote many books and thousands of pages of magazine articles, for which she received pay.

Dale Carnegie, who teaches men of affairs how to express their thoughts in public, has written books on public speaking. According to Ripley, Mr. Carnegie, who has listened to and critized more talks by adults than any other living man, was a total failure the first half dozen times he attempted to speak in public.

He was born on a farm ten miles from a railroad down in Missouri. In his boyhood he worked for five cents an hour picking berries and cutting weeds. There were floods, crop failures, and one catastrophe after another on the farm, and on several occasions the bank threatened to foreclose the mortgage. The family moved to another farm at Warrensburg, Missouri. In this town there was a college, and after milking the cows, feeding the hogs, cutting the family wood, each morning, Dale rode a mule three miles to school, and after riding home in the evening, did the chores again, and studied at night by coal-oil lamps. Of the hundreds of students in this State Teachers' College, Carnegie was one of a very few who were too poor to board in the town. Later he spent his time training executives—not at five cents an hour, but at a dollar a minute. His books are among the best sellers.

So we might go on calling the roll of the good and great. They have all had their struggles, their hardships, their disappointments. If you have no head winds to fight against, you will be an exception. It is well to remember what Longfellow has said:

> Heights by great men reached and kept.
> Were not attained by sudden flight,
> But they, while their companions slept,
> Were toiling upward in the night."

Two Glasses of Milk

IT WAS a sultry afternoon in midsummer many years ago and before the automobile had been invented. A famous surgeon was riding his bicycle along a country road. The way was rough and dusty, and the afternoon sun beamed down with intense heat. Looking some distance ahead, the perspiring traveler noticed a neat, cozy cottage nestled among some inviting shade trees near the road. And as he neared the place, he noticed a well, with a bucket, and a dipper hanging near by. The cool shade and the prospect of a refreshing drink urged him to turn in at the gate, which he did.

A young woman, busy with her mending, was seated on the porch. She arose and greeted the stranger, who inquired if he might have a cold drink.

"Certainly you may," she said in the kindest voice possible, "but wouldn't you rather have a drink of cold milk? We have lots of it on the ice, and if you would care for it, I shall be glad to get some for you. It is nourishing as well as refreshing, and riding a wheel on such a hot day is hard work."

"That would surely be a treat," answered the caller, "but I would not want to bother you. I fear I would be imposing on your kindness and generosity."

It was no imposition to this graceful young lady, who was eager to be of help to the passing stranger. She hurried to the ice house, and returned with a pitcher of rich, cold milk. The doctor drank two glasses, and felt much refreshed for his journey. The young woman urged him to rest awhile under the friendly trees, and he en-

Only a smile and two glasses of milk, but how valuable they proved to be.

joyed a few moments in the cool of the shade before going on his way. From the depths of his heart he told the
young woman how much her unexpected kindness had
meant to him, and as he departed, handed her his card,
saying, "If you ever come to the city and need the advice of a physician, please call on me."

The weeks and the months rolled by, and this inci-
dent had been forgotten by the young lady and her parents. Many a stranger had been helped on his way by
these kindly people; so why should they remember such
kindnesses?

About a year later the mother became seriously ill,
and the family physician advised that she go to the city
at once for an operation. They were poor, and this was
discouraging news for them. The mother said that
there was no use in their even thinking of it, for they
could not afford to pay the surgeon and the hospital
their fees. But the father and the daughter insisted
that she must go, and began immediately to plan ways
and means of saving money to pay the expenses. It was
the only way for mother to regain her health.

In a few days they were ready for the trip. The
mother was to go to the hospital, and the daughter
would stay with an aunt who lived in the city. While
she was packing the trunk the card which the doctor
had given her some months before fell from among her
trinkets. Immediately she decided that she would hunt
for him upon arrival in the city. Hadn't he said to be
sure to look him up if they should ever need the advice
of a physician?

So, before choosing the hospital to which her mother should go, she sought the home of this kind stranger
to ask his advice. She was just a little embarrassed

when she was shown into the beautiful office of this well
known surgeon. But his pleasant face and hearty hand-
shake set her at ease. He had not forgotten the kindness
shown him on that hot summer afternoon some months
before.

The young lady explained all that the family physician in the country had said about her mother, and
then asked the surgeon which hospital he thought
would be best for her mother.

"My dear girl," said the big-hearted physician, "if
you will leave your mother with me, I will give her the
best care I know how. I have a sanitarium of my own,
and will personally attend your mother. I will treat her
as I would my own mother. You may come to see her
every day. Of course, you don't know me, and if there
are any doubts in your mind, you might get in touch
with your own family doctor at home and ask him about
me."

So the mother was taken to the sanitarium of the famous surgeon.

When the young lady told her aunt where she had
taken her mother, the aunt was alarmed. "My child,"
she said, "don't you know that this surgeon charges
exorbitant prices? He gets as much as a $1,000 for an
operation, and the charge for board and nursing in his
private sanitarium will be terrible. Your poor father
cannot afford to pay such prices. You have made a
mistake, I fear.'

This frightened the girl. She had never had any experience with hospitals and surgeons, and this worry
about the expenses, along with the anxiety about her
mother, drove her to tears. She went to her room and
had a good cry. But down in her heart she felt that the

surgeon would not be unreasonable. She could not forget his kind face and pleasant smile.

The operation was successful, and each day when the young lady visited the mother, she found her stronger. One day the doctor said that mother might go home in two weeks. This would make a stay of four weeks in the sanitarium. The girl was happy at the thought of the family being together at home again, but anxious about the expenses. How would father ever be able to pay for them?

The day arrived when mother was to start for home. Father had come to the city, and he and the mother and the daughter were in the office of the doctor. The patient was well and happy. She looked better than she had looked for a long time. And the father and the daughter were happy, too, to know that the operation was over and that the mother would soon be her old self again. But the daughter kept thinking of the bill that the surgeon would give them, and wondering how it could be paid.

Shaking hands with them, the surgeon said to the mother, "I am surely happy to see that you are all right again. I hope your visit has done you good that will last. It has been a pleasure to be of help to you. I have made out your bill and placed it in this envelope, and I am going to ask that you do not open it until you get home tonight. After supper is over, and the work is done, and you are all together in the sitting room, open up the envelope and talk the matter over."

The family tried their best to express their thanks to the doctor for helping the mother to get back her health, and then left for home. They could hardly wait until evening to open up the envelope. The daughter

was more fearful than curious. That night father
opened the envelope and read aloud the statement. This
is what he read:

> "Professional services $1,000
> Nursing and hospital care 200
> $1,200

"Received payment in full by two glasses of milk,
furnished a weary traveler on a hot summer day."

The incidents related in this story really happened
a good many years ago, but it is just as true today as
then that kindness costs little and pays big dividends.
Little words and deeds of kindness may lighten some
one's load and bring joy to both the giver and the receiver.

Keep the Oil Can Handy

I DROVE a squeaking car into the garage the other day. Those squeaks don't mean anything serious, but they do get on our nerves.

"Charley," I inquired of the mechanic, "what can I do to this car so it will not begin to squeak after it has been driven four or five hundred miles?"

He smiled in an amused sort of way, as if I had asked a very foolish or childish question. "Well, sir," he replied, "the best thing I know to do is just to keep it well oiled and greased."

So every few hundred miles I have the springs sprayed with oil, and the squeaks disappear. A little oil has the same magic effect on my office chair or a squeaking door.

There are so many things to irritate us today. Life is tense and strenuous. We are so highly geared and drive so rapidly that we don't go far until the squeaks appear—little things which may not be serious but which get on our nerves. They annoy and trouble us.

A button is off our clean shirt, and it upsets us. Such a trifling thing should not bother a big, husky man, but it seems to. Instead of pouring a little oil on the waters, we really use gasoline and virtually set a match to it. That same shirt may have all the buttons on 364 days in the year and we never utter one word of praise, but when we find a button gone on the 365th morning, we rave and storm. Keep an oil can handy for such occasions.

Hubby is late to dinner—the souffle has fallen, and

Lives, like ships, are not unsinkable.

the potatoes have been ruined by standing too long. To fret and stew and fume does not improve the meal—it may retard digestion. Almost any man would rather go without dinner than to have his wife disgruntled and unhappy.

When the *Titanic* went down, the *Carpathia* rushed to her assistance. As she steamed toward the sinking liner, the captain ordered that barrels of oil be in readiness, that they might be poured on the waters of the old Atlantic when they came near the *Titanic*. They made free use of oil, which calmed the waters of the ocean and made less difficult the work of rescue. It is said that a drop of oil will cover a whole square mile of sea surface. It seems almost unbelievable.

Life's ocean is dotted with ships, large and small. Some, sailing in confidence and security and supposed to be "unsinkable," as was the great *Titanic,* may as suddenly find themselves in distress. Some, pleasure-bound, have expected no storm on life's sea. Others may not have estimated the power of wind and wave correctly, and have not prepared for the journey. Many derelicts are on the sea, with neither chart nor compass, a menace to themselves and to others.

Today we find life's ocean is stormy. All about us are trouble and distress. Many a bark is about to be swallowed up by the waves of affliction, sorrow, grief, suffering, temptation, and trial. Let us bear in mind that a little oil will cover a large surface. A kind word, a cheery smile, a helping hand, just a little act of kindness may help some one through the storm. We, too, may strike stormy seas and need a helping hand.

Let us use the oil can freely in our homes, and help our own loved ones through the squalls which come

now and then. It won't take much oil to keep the home
waters calm and untroubled. Then let us use more oil
that it may extend to our neighborhoods, that our neighbors, who may be storm tossed, may have smoother seas.
And wherever we find a fellow mariner in distress, let
us pour on freely the oil of love and brotherly kindness.

Prayer -- Is It Out of Date?

IF YOU were crossing the Atlantic in one of our modern liners, and the great vessel struck an iceberg, and you were forced to put on a life preserver and jump into the icy waters of the turbulent old ocean in an endeavor to save your life, would you pray?

If you were near death's door, and the doctor told you there was no hope, would you ask the Lord to spare your life? If you were out of work and in dire need of life's necessities, would you have faith enough to get down on your knees and ask God for help? If you had lost your watch or fountain pen, would you make that a matter of prayer? If the coal bin was empty, would you pray for coal? If you were at the fork in the road, and did not know which way to take, would you ask the Lord to help you in making the decision?

Do you feel that prayer is out of date, and would be just so much time wasted? Has your faith weakened in these days of skepticism and unbelief?

Not long ago Mr. Markey, a literary man, set out in his Ford to test the faith of the American people. He drove 16,000 miles, and interviewed some 500 men and women from the common walks of life. He asked these people if they were getting anything from their religion in these times of stress. Was it, he questioned, any prop to them? Was their faith in God and His word any help in meeting the trials of every day? Only one man in 500 said that his religion, his faith in God, was a real help. The rest had little or no faith, no hope, no trust in God. "Everywhere," says Mr. Markey, "I en-

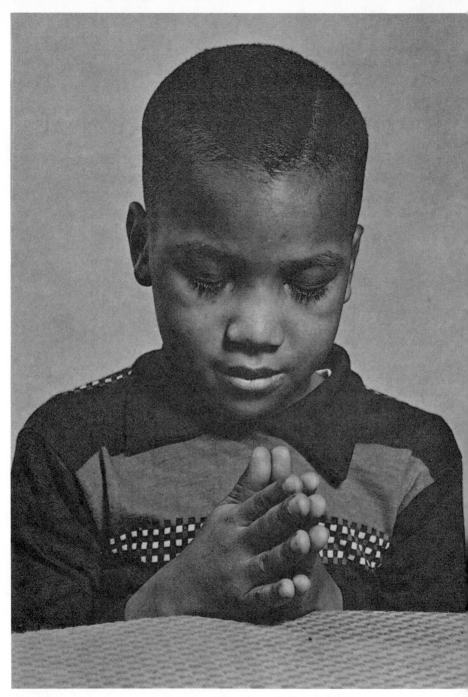

Prayer is like talking to one's best friend.

countered skepticism, distrust, or amusement at the be-
liefs of our fathers."

And he came to the conclusion that "Christianity
is hardly to be considered at all as a force in American
life, in directing its current or its desires."

In these times of stress and strain, do you find yourself one of this growing army of unbelievers, with no
faith and no hope? Or in a time of emergency would
you do as did a friend of mine, a minister of the gospel,
when he found himself in a tight place not long ago? He
and his wife and little boy had moved into the town of
Leader, Saskatchewan, at the request of the conference
committee. They rented a house, and proceeded to un-
pack their household goods. The first day was a busy
one, and Mrs. Berg did not notice until bedtime that
they were out of bread, and that they had no flour with
which to bake. She told her husband that they needed
flour, and he told her that he did not have a cent of
money left. They were strangers in the town, and he
did not like to ask the merchants for credit. What could
they do? As they knelt around the family altar before
retiring, they told the Lord their need, and asked Him
to provide for them in His own way.

Early next morning Mrs. Berg opened the front
door, and there on the porch, leaning against one of the
posts, was 100 pounds of Five Roses Flour. They made
inquiries of the merchants and others, but could not find
out who put the flour on the porch. They were sure of
one thing, however, that God had sent it in answer to
their prayers, for they had not mentioned their need to
any one else.

In these days of skepticism and doubt there are
many who have no faith in God and His word, and na-

turally they consider prayer useless and even foolish.
We are living in the time referred to by the Saviour
when He said, "Nevertheless when the Son of man cometh, shall He find faith on the earth?" Luke 18:8.

Suppose you were crossing the ocean to meet an appointment on the other side, and when your vessel was
in mid-ocean, it ran into a heavy fog and was delayed
so much that the captain told you you would reach port
twenty-four hours late; would you pray about it?
George Muller did.

This man of faith was crossing the Atlantic Ocean
from east to west, headed for Quebec City, where he had
an important engagement for a definite time. In mid-
Atlantic a dense, heavy fog settled down, and the engines had to be slowed until the ship barely crept along.
Mr. Muller told the captain of his appointment, and
asked if the ship might be speeded up a bit. But the
captain told him this would be suicide, and that he
would not dare to risk the lives of the many passengers
on board. "But," said Mr. Muller, "I must be in Quebec on Saturday night."

"It is out of the question," the captain answered.

Then Mr. Muller asked the captain if he would go
into one of the cabins with him and pray about the matter. They would ask the Lord to see that the fog lifted,
so they could speed up the engines and get to Quebec in
time for Mr. Muller's appointment. The captain was
willing. Mr. Muller prayed a simple, earnest prayer,
telling the Lord about his plans and the urgency of his
being in Quebec on Saturday night.

The captain was about to pray too, when Mr. Muller
interrupted: "You don't need to pray, captain, for in
the first place, you don't believe that God will lift the

fog; and in the second place, you don't need to pray, for God has already answered my prayer."

They arose from their knees and went on deck. The fog had lifted, and they were soon sailing full speed ahead, and reached Quebec in time for Mr. Muller's appointment.

Before his death, this man of faith declared that he had had at least 50,000 definite answers to prayer. During his long and useful life, more than 10,000 orphans were cared for in the orphanages which he established without any money of his own, and which were maintained entirely as the result of prayer. When he decided to build the first shelter for boys and girls, he told the Lord of his plans, and the money came to him without his soliciting any one for help. Other orphanages were built, and the Lord supplied the food, fuel, and clothing needed in caring for thousands of boys and girls, in answer to Mr. Muller's prayers.

He did not at any time tell any one of the needs of these institutions, nor would he permit any of his helpers to do so. They did not borrow nor go into debt. They just told the Lord their needs, and He answered their prayers.

Often, when the evening meal was finished, there was no food on hand for breakfast, but food was sure to arrive before time for the morning meal. In all his journals he tells of only one instance where it was necessary for them to delay a meal, and that was only for a half hour. One morning there was just enough food for breakfast, but before noon the postman came with a letter from far-off India, and in it was $250. One other morning there was only five cents left in the treasury, but at eleven o'clock a gift of twenty-seven dollars came in, and this supplied the needed midday meal.

One cold winter day Mr. Muller was told that the boiler which supplied the heat for one of the buildings would have to be repaired, and that the fire would have to be out for sometime. There were 300 children in this building, and they must be kept warm. What could they do? Mr. Muller asked the Lord to send them a south wind and warm weather, so the children would not suffer from the cold while the fire was out. They decided to do the work on a certain day. The day before was bitterly cold, and a strong wind was blowing from the north. During the night the wind shifted to the south, and all the time they were working on the furnace a warm, balmy breeze blew from that quarter, and the weather was so mild that no fire was needed. Did this just happen?

Some one suggested to Mr. Muller that on this plan of working, he lived from hand to mouth. "Yes," he replied, "that is true. It is God's hand and my mouth."

Was God partial to Mr. Muller? Will He do as much for you and me? He will if we comply with the conditions.

Positive Proof

IN A CERTAIN town lived a prosperous wood dealer whose business had begun to dwindle. Once he was popular and prosperous. But now business had begun to fall off, and he had come to be classed as a shrewd, mean, dishonest man. Here is how it happened. For a time his business had grown, and he was making enough money for himself and family, and had some to put in the bank each week. Greedy for larger profits, he decided to cut his logs of wood a few inches shorter than the required length. Naturally, people did not want to deal with him.

A cord of wood was supposed to be four feet in length. But he instructed his men to make it three feet and seven inches. He felt no one would notice that the logs were shorter, and in the course of a year it would mean hundreds of dollars for his bank account.

But customers measured the wood, and the story spread through the community that the wood dealer was dishonest. People refused to buy from him; they preferred to deal with an honest man.

One day, to the surprise of all, it was reported that this man had been converted—had become a Christian. Not many believed the report, for they felt he was beyond any help.

His name was being discussed by a group of men in one of the town's grocery stores. One of the men slipped away from the group for a few minutes. He soon returned and excitedly exclaimed, "It's true boys! He's converted, all right! It's true!"

A minister talks about Christianity. But people believe more the person who lives it.

Almost in concert they asked, "How do you know? Where did you get your information?"

"Why, I slipped out and measured the wood he cut yesterday, and it is a full four feet long!"

That was enough. They doubted no more. His conversion was genuine.

And after all, isn't that the best yardstick to apply to any person's religion? The Master Himself said, "Ye shall know them by their fruits." Matthew 7:16. The fact that your name is on the register of some popular church is no guarantee of your conversion, your sincerity. You may belong to the biggest church in your town and still be a hypocrite.

A minister was once preaching on the blessings which come into the life, into the home, and into the community through real, practical Christianity. He mentioned the virtues which would be seen in the life of a Christian. He pictured a home where the principles of Christianity were interwoven with all the daily duties and transactions of the home.

A lady in the pews whispered to her seatmate. "That is a beautiful picture, but I wonder if he lives this life himself."

"I am happy to tell you he does," replied the woman, "for I happen to be his wife. He lives what he preaches."

That is what our old world needs today—more laymembers, and preachers, too, who really live their creeds. How many of our lodges and secret orders have beautiful ideals incorporated in their by-laws. Perhaps not one member in a hundred knows what his organization stands for. The Christian church has standards given us by the Master Himself. There is nothing wrong with the standards.   What we need is to live up to them.

Ask any church member today just what his church believes, and see what answer you get. I have tried it, and found out that most of these people, if honest, will tell you they don't know.   Now and then you will find someone who really knows what he believes.

If the standards as given us by the Master were lived by every professing Christian today, this would be a much better world in which to live.

Helen's Secret

HELEN, Margaret, and their mother were keeping a secret. Although their father did not know what the girls were about, he saw that every day they were busy at washing, ironing, sewing, housework, and cooking. There were other tasks over the week end. During summer vacation they worked all day.

They were not working for new dresses, a social event, or anything of the sort. All of the activity was a very special secret.

All of the money was saved in the same place. But it was a very odd kind of bank. You would never guess where they kept their coins! It was in the back of their old upright piano. When someone paid them for laundry, or for running errands, they would take out just the little that they needed immediately, and the rest went in the back of the piano.

They were saving to go away to boarding school. In their town a young person could not go beyond twelve grades in school. If he would secure more education, it had to be obtained elsewhere. So both girls were planning to go away to boarding school.

Their father thought that it was useless to give girls an advanced education. He thought that such money would be wasted. Neither the girls nor their mother could change his mind. Seeing that argument would do no good, they wrote for a catalog, decided on the expenses for one year, and started right in to secure the necessary money.

August came. School would be starting in just

about another month. Helen, Margaret, and their mother were still working. They were still keeping their secret.

One day the two girls and their mother decided to take all of the money from the piano, count it, and find how much more was needed.

Father was away when this great moment arrived. Perhaps he had gone around the corner to exchange a few words with his good friend the ice vendor.

With the door securely locked and the shades carefully drawn, the girls and their mother pulled the piano

Girls like sharing secrets.

from the wall and removed the stocking in which the funds were stored away. Pennies, nickels, dimes, quarters, and half dollars were carefully stacked. The few bills were placed in another pile. Mother stood watch at the door.

When all the counting was done, the girls found that they did not have as much money as they had thought. There was enough for one to go away to school, but not enough for two. One of the girls would have to stay behind.

"Suppose you go, Margaret," Helen said. "I'll stay here and work again this year."

"No, you must go," Margaret responded quietly. "I have my job here, and Mother and I have already talked it over. You go first. In a year or two you will be teaching in a small school. Then I can go."

For Helen there seemed no other choice. Her sister and her mother had already settled the matter when she was not around. With a sad feeling, therefore, she went off to boarding school. Under those conditions she had to do an exceptional job with her school work.

The father was completely surprised when he found out what they were doing. Although he had expressed himself as being unfavorable to the idea of educating girls, he was now glad to see his daughter going away to school.

Helen soon found herself in front of the girl's dormitory at the boarding school. There were new faces everywhere. She eagerly joined them in discussing the courses which they planned to take.

There was a hospital on the grounds also. To her surprise she discovered that the girls who were planning for nurses' training did not have to pay nearly as much money. There was only a small fee to pay at the beginning, and their work at the hospital took care of the rest.

This was an idea. She would take the nursing course instead of the teaching course. She had always liked nursing anyway. Then Margaret also could come to boarding school and take up her work as a teacher. She could hardly wait to write the good news home!

In an unusual way their dreams had come true. Their secret bank in the old piano had yielded an education for both Helen and Margaret.

Those Little Deeds Well Done

D ID YOU ever notice a news agent going through the train picking up papers which he had previously sold to customers, and which they had discarded after having read them? I wonder if you thought the same as I thought when I watched one of these men recently. He was going from seat to seat, picking up papers, smoothing them out just a little, and piling them on his arm. I supposed, of course, that he planned to take them into the next coach, straighten them up, and sell them again, thus adding a few more pennies to his slender income.

While I felt he might need the money, he dropped just a little in my estimation, when I thought of his reselling those old papers to passengers. "There are tricks in all trades," I said to myself, and felt that he must be rather a little soul to do such things. I must admit, however, that as he picked up those straggling pages the man had an expression of joy on his face, and a light in his eye, which do not originate in a dwarfed soul. I judged him from outward appearances. I surmised something and drew my own conclusions.

I followed him into the next coach and watched him arranging and folding those papers. He piled them neatly in a pile, rolled them up and tied a string around them. I asked if they had any value, and then he told me the secret.

"There is an old man living in a little shack up the line here a piece," he said. "He has lived out here all alone for years and years. He has no company, and I

The train rolled on, . . . and on it was a man whose heart was glad because of a little act of kindness done to a fellowman.

guess the days and nights get pretty long. He is miles from town, and there are no roads into the district. Every time I come by I throw him a roll of papers."

I have thought of his reply a good many times since. "Well, Mac," he answered, "many people haven't learned how to live yet. It doesn't cost me anything to gather up these old papers, and it brings a great deal of joy and sunshine to this lonely old man. We can get much out of life ourselves by doing just little things for others as we go along."

I went out in the vestibule with him and watched for the little cabin and the lonely old man. Sure enough, he was out by the track waiting. And I wish that I might have gotten a picture of the old gentleman's face; yes—and of the newsie's countenance also, when the papers changed hands. The train rolled on its way down the mountains toward the great Pacific, and on it was a man whose heart was glad because of a little act of kindness done to a fellow man.

And on that train was one man who said to himself that he should not judge people too quickly from outward appearances, and that after all, much of the joy of life comes from doing little acts and deeds of kindness for which he expects no similar returns.

The organ makes beautiful music.

How John Bought the Organ

HOW MUCH is that organ, sir?" asked a little boy of a dealer in secondhand furniture.

"Thirty-five dollars, Sonny," was the reply.

The little fellow had looked in every store in the city, hoping to find some instrument that he might even dream of buying. His eyes sparkled with real joy when he learned the price. He did not have a cent, but he felt sure that he and his mother could arrange some way to buy this organ. He thought to himself: "Thirty-five dollars isn't much for a *real* organ. How I wish Mother would buy it for me! I am going to ask her."

John's mother was a widow, and she found it difficult to buy food and clothing for herself and her boy. So she was not very enthusiastic about his bargain. He had teased her day after day for a musical instrument, and she had wished and hoped that in some way she might make his dreams come true. He told his story confidently, but his mother had to say, "No."

But John couldn't forget about the organ, and talked about it in the morning, at noon, and at night. He dreamed about it too. Each day he went by the store to see if it was still there.

One day when he was teasing and begging his mother, she happened to have five dollars. To her this was a large sum, and there were many places waiting for it. But she was so tired of having to say, "No," to John that she gave him the money, and told him he might buy the organ if he could get it for the five dollars.

John lost no time in getting to the store. He talked the matter over frankly with the owner. The gentleman told him that he might take the organ home and pay the rest of it when he could. How happy he was, no one will ever know! The organ was sent out, and the little fellow was there to receive it. While he was exceedingly happy, his mother was worried, for she wondered how the rest of the money would ever be paid. She did not wish to mar his pleasure. So she went back to her work, without telling him how she felt.

Soon she heard the most beautiful music coming from the room, and wondered whom John could have found to play so well. She silently tiptoed into the room. Imagine her surprise to find her own John, bent lovingly over the keyboard, expressing his happiness through the old organ!

She stood and listened, and John played on, for he was so absorbed in his music that he didn't notice that she had come in. He had not had even one lesson, and the mother knew now that John possessed a great gift, and that she must help him to develop it.

There were many days of toil and sacrifice before the organ was paid for. John spent every moment possible in practice, and friends who recognized his unusual ability helped him to go to school. It wasn't long until he could play well enough to give lessons to others, and he began to earn something himself. In the years that followed he studied under some great teachers, and was finally recognized as great by the State of South Carolina. They asked him to play at the dedication of the organ at the State College. Later he became assistant organist, and was granted the degree of Master of Arts in music.

The name of John Donovan Moore is known far and near today, and his students are found in many parts of the country. One of them is William Sandford Lawrence, accompanist of Roland Hayes, the noted tenor.

John bought his mother a comfortable home in the South, for she had first place in his heart. "I love my music," he said, "but it must take second place in my life. Mother comes first of all." Thus he tried to repay her for her years of hard work and sacrifice for him.

Yellow Roses

TWO BOYS and a girl about ten years old, ragged, but with clean hands and faces, stepped into a florist's shop one bright, sunny afternoon. From their deportment one would have judged that their errand was one of importance, for there was a serious look on their faces. The boys had removed their hats, and one of them, acting as spokesman, approaching a salesman, said, "We're the committee, and we'd like some nice yellow flowers."

The florist sized up his customers and offered them some inexpensive blossoms.

"I think we'd like something better than that."

"Must they be yellow?" the salesman inquired.

"Yes, sir," the little fellow replied. "You see, mister, Mickey would like'm better if they were yellow, because Mickey had a yellow sweater."

When asked if the flowers were for a funeral, the spokesman of the committee nodded and made an attempt to speak. Tears had already appeared in the little girl's eyes and were running down her cheeks. "She's his sister," the boy said. "Mickey was a good kid. A truck—just yesterday—we was playing a game in the street. We saw it happen, but there was nothing we could do." His eyes were moist by this time, and his voice atremble.

Then the other boy took up the thread of the story, "Us kids took up a collection, we got eighteen cents. Would—would roses cost an awful lot, mister? Nice yellow roses?"

The big hearted florist sensed the situation. "I have some nice yellow roses here," he said, "that I'm selling for eighteen cents a dozen," and showed them to the committee.

"Those will be great," said one of the boys.

"Yes, Mickey would love those," the other added.

"All right," said the florist, "I will make up a nice spray, and put some ferns in it and a pretty ribbon around it. Where shall I send it for you?"

"If you don't mind, Mister, we'd like to take them with us. We would kind'a like to take them over—and—sort of give them to Mickey ourselves. He would like it better that way."

The spray was quickly arranged, the eighteen cents paid, and the happy though sorrowing youngsters hurried off to give the yellow roses to Mickey.

The sad part of this story is that poor Mickey didn't know of their love and affection. He didn't see the tear-reddened eyes, hear the choking words, or enjoy the beautiful yellow roses. He went through life without the flowers.

Nothing is too good for our loved ones after they are gone. Kind words are freely given, their good deeds told again and again, their virtues repeated over and over. And many of these dear ones, who had not one bouquet during life, are showered with the best the florists produce after it has slipped from them.

It is a beautiful custom to buy flowers when a loved one is called in death, but why wait until the funeral to give flowers? Why not resolve to pass out a few bouquets to our dear ones, our friends, while they can enjoy them? Magnify the virtues in them now, tell of their good qualities, say the kind words, yes, even buy flowers.

The boys talked about trains and planes.

Jimmy's Wish

OUR TRAIN was winding its way through the Kicking Horse Pass, in the Canadian Rockies. I had reveled in the beauties of those mighty mountains almost to the point of saturation, then read for a while, and fell into a conversation with a little man of about twelve years of age, who was traveling alone from Calgary to Vancouver. He was a manly little fellow, full of life, and unusually courteous.

We talked of trains, boats, airplanes, and other things in which boys are usually interested. He was working on a model plane as we traveled along. Every now and then he would take it in one hand and zoom it through space, his face expressing more than I can tell on paper.

He had suggested several subjects of conversation —topics of interest to his boyish heart. But imagine my surprise when he looked up at me with a real earnestness in his face, and said, "I wish my whiskers would hurry and grow."

"Well, Jimmy," I said, "that won't be long now. They will come all too soon. And some day you will be wishing you did not have to shave every day."

By the look in his eye, I know he doubted what I said.

How many boys have had this same feeling, and when the whiskers did grow and they had to shave every day, come what may, they discovered that their wish had been a very foolish one.

How many, many things we wish we had, and how

many foolish desires are hidden in our hearts! We are all children grown tall.

When driving to the West Coast not long ago, it seemed to me that all of California was leaving the state —headed for the country from which I had come. I was going to California with a happy heart, and with hearts just as light they were going to the East.

Many a poor man today is longing to be rich, and many a rich man is thinking of the real joys he knew in the days before he had accumulated wealth. He then had real true friends. Days of toil brought a keen appetite and a good night's rest at the close of the busy day. The rich man has found that dollars alone don't bring happiness.

It is a good thing that joy does not depend on the possession of whiskers or dollars, or other temporal things. Happiness comes from the inside and not from the outside. Of course, the inside may be influenced by these very real things which surround us. But even though there may be greater joys in anticipation than in reality, the disappointments should not sour us on life. When the whiskers come, we might as well get as much happiness as possible out of that morning shave. And if there is not as much fun in taking care of real babies as there was in playing with dolls in those make-believe days, why not pack as much joy as possible into those precious days when the children must be kissed and cuddled and bathed? It may have been more fun to play at keeping house than there is in dusting, and cleaning, and washing dirty dishes. But we may find some pleasure, some joy, even in the menial tasks of every day—so much that they can cease to be drudgery?

I was struggling with my old grip the other day,

trying to pack into it more than it was intended to hold, so I could go another 500 miles farther from home, and a girl in her teens was watching me with a rather envious eye. I knew what was in her heart. I had been a junior myself. Finally she expressed the desire which I knew was there, saying: "You are lucky, aren't you? I wish I could take a long trip somewhere."

Any normal person has had those longings, I suppose. But when I had taken some long, long trips, I learned a great deal. Yet, while I would prefer to stay home and let someone else get disillusioned, I do try to get all the happiness I can out of the necessary trips. Why not?

Many of our joys are greater in our dreams than in reality. And I am glad this is true of our troubles, too. Life is just about what we make it.

The tenant farmer had to reap the harvest of his anger.

A Foolish Farmer

A TENANT farmer had lived on a certain farm for a good many years, renewing his lease from time to time as it expired. Day by day he had been up at dawn, and worked after other men had gone to bed at night. He had fertilized and built up the soil. The fences had been kept in good repair. He had struggled valiantly to keep down the weeds. The buildings were well painted and in good condition. The orchard had been trimmed and sprayed annually, and bore the best fruit in the neighborhood. In short, it was a model farm, admired by farmers far and near.

One day the agent who looked after the land called on the farmer and notified him that he would have to vacate the place. The owner's son, who was about to be married, wanted to take over the farm.

It is not difficult to imagine some of the feelings of this hard-working farmer. He made a number of offers to the owner, hoping that he might change his mind. But all his suggestions were in vain. The day was set when he must leave the place, and it seemed to him that the labor of the years had been lost to him.

In the weeks that intervened he had done some angry brooding, and had decided to get revenge. He gathered weed seeds wherever they could be found, seeds which were the pest of the farmer, and just before he was to leave the place, one dark night he moved up and down over the clean fertile fields, sowing broadcast the seeds of the noxious weeds.

The next morning, bright and early, while the farmer was still doing the chores, the agent drove up.   He promptly passed on the information that the owner's plans had been changed—the son had decided not to move onto the farm, and the lease could be renewed.

"What a fool I've been," the farmer exclaimed. Just what he meant the agent never knew. But the farmer knew that he would have to reap from his sowing. He knew of the hours of toil and anguish he must spend because of that one night's deed.

You and I must reap as we sow. If we sow wild oats, we cannot expect to reap the tame variety. If we sow frowns and cross words, we may expect people to shun us. Unkind criticism and backbiting won't make us friends nor bring us joy. Days of toil for ourselves alone will not give us happiness. Plant kindness, courtesy, helpfulness, and you will have a joyous reaping. It is one of God's laws, "Whatsoever a man soweth, that shall he also reap.' Galatians 6:7.

And someday we will be asked to vacate the place, to go the way of all the earth. In the day of final awards, the time of reaping, you and I shall reap as we have sown. May we sow wisely.

Troubles

IN HIS autobiography, *Man and Rubber,* Harvey S. Firestone tells an interesting little story which particularly concerns Henry Ford, who had been his close personal friend.

Thomas Edison, John Burroughs, Mr. Ford, and Mr. Firestone were on one of their summer camping trips, and were traveling by automobile. They were camped one evening near the road, and saw a man walking briskly down the highway toward them. On approaching the group, he said, "Gentlemen, I'm in trouble up the road about a mile. I am on my way to an important engagement, and my car has stalled. It absolutely refuses to go. Do any of you men know anything about a Ford?"

Mr. Firestone answered his query. Pointing to Mr. Ford, he said, "That old fellow over there knows quite a bit about a Ford car."

"Will you come and help me?" the man asked pleadingly.

"With pleasure," Mr. Ford replied.

Mr. Ford started up the Model T which he happened to be driving, and he and the stranger drove back to the stalled car. In a few minutes he had the man's car purring, and both Mr. Ford and the stranger were happy.

"How much do I owe you?" asked the man, taking out his purse.

"Nothing at all," cheerfully replied the wealthy automobile manufacturer.

"It is worth a lot to me to be able to get on my way. And you have fixed my car so that it runs better than it ever ran before. I would like to show you that I appreciate what you have done for me," stated the befriended one.

"It is sufficient reward for me to be able to be of some help to you," replied the automobile manufacturer.

"I certainly do thank you, and do you mind if I say this. If I knew as much about an automobile as you know, I would not be riding around in a thing like that," said the other, pointing to Mr. Ford's Model T.

Mr. Ford drove back to his friends, told the story, and they all had a hearty laugh.

The man who had designed and made the car understood its every part. He could make it alive when it had gone dead. He made it run as it had never run before.

With you and me things often go wrong. We make mistakes, our plans don't work. We slip and fall. Sometimes we seem to be sliding back instead of making progress. Our acquaintances think they know the trouble and they suggest this remedy and that, but still things don't go right.

There is One who knows about your weakness and mine, for He has gone over the way before us. He is our Creator, our Maker. Why shouldn't He know more about us and our needs than any other? Why shouldn't we go to Him with our troubles and trials? He has invited us to come.

Mother's Furrows

A TALL sailor stood in front of the gate addressing the group of admirers. "Boys," he said, "I have been trying every day for the last two years to straighten out some furrows, and I cannot do it."

He noticed one of the boys turn to look at his lawn and his small garden.

"Oh," he explained quickly, "I do not mean that kind of furrow, my boy. "It is not a land furrow that I have been trying to straighten."

He looked away into space as he continued to talk. "When I was a boy, I was somewhat wayward and a little wild. My mother used to plead with me, pray with me, and punish me. My father was dead, making it all the more difficult for her, but she was never impatient. How she bore all my stubborn ways with such patience will always be a mystery to me. I knew that she was anxious about me, and I knew that it was making changes in her face, making it look careworn and old. After a few years I was tired of all restraint. I ran away and went off to sea. I had a rough time at first. Still I liked the water, and I liked the traveling from place to place.

"Then I decided to stay overseas for a while, and I started a little business. About this time I began enclosing a little money in my letters to Mother. She always wrote me beautiful letters in answer during those years I was away. Then the letters grew longer, and I knew that she longed for the son who tried her patience so. I began to long for my mother also.

Mothers work hard for their families.

"When I could stand it no longer, I came back. Such a welcome she gave me! She seemed so surprised at my return.

"Mother is not a very old woman, boys," the sailor went on, "but the first thing I noticed was the gray in her hair and the furrows on her brow. I knew I had helped to turn the color of her hair. I had also drawn those lines in that forehead that was otherwise smooth. Those are the furrows, boys, that I have been trying to straighten.

"But last night, Mother fell asleep in her chair; and I have been thinking it all over, trying to determine what progress I had made. Her face was very peaceful, and her expression seemed very contented, but those furrows are still there. I have not succeeded in straightening them out. I do not believe now that I ever shall.

"Until her death, Mother will have furrows on her brow. I think it is a good piece of advice to pass on to you, that if you disregard your parents' counsel now, and cause them trouble, their grief will abide, my lads, it will abide!"

"But sailor," broke in one of the boys, with a troubled countenance, "I should think that if you are so kind and good now, it need not matter so much!"

"Ah, Freddie," said the strong man, "you cannot undo the past. You may do much to atone for it, you may do much to make the rough path smooth, but you cannot straighten out the old furrows; remember that."

"Guess I'll go and chop some wood for Mother. I had almost forgotten," said Jimmy in an unusually quiet tone.

"Yes, and I have some errands to do," suddenly remembered Billy.

"Touched and taken!" said the kindly sailor to himself, as the boys tramped off.

Billy's mother declared two weeks afterward that
Billy was "really getting to be a comfort!" And Jimmy's mother, meeting the sailor about that time, remarked that her boy always meant to be a good boy, but
now he was actually being one.

"Your stories that they like so much have good
morals in them now and then," added the gratified
mother, with a smile.

The sailor watched her until she was out of sight.
Then with folded arms, he said softly to himself,
"Well, I shall be thankful if a word of mine will help
the boys to keep furrows from their mothers' brows.
Once there, it is a difficult task to straighten them out."

What Made Him a Tramp?

A LADY of refinement, when conversing with a "knight of the road," a hobo, inquired about his habits. "How," asked the lady, "do you decide where your next journey shall take you? What enters into your decision? How do you determine whether you shall travel to Alaska or to New Orleans?

"I always turn my back to the wind," the tramp replied. "If the wind is from the east I go west. If it is from the north, I go south."

That was what made him a hobo. He did not have the courage or backbone to face the wind, and push on in its teeth. There are multitudes today who won't face the wind, and who won't pull against the stream. They can't stand alone, and they don't care to struggle, to put forth an effort.

To travel with the crowd is the path of least resistance. Not many today have the courage to stand alone.

Samuel F. B. Morse, a young man who had invented an instrument that could send a message over wires, tried to interest the United States Congress in building an experimental line to test out his idea. They told Morse that they might as well appropriate money to build a railroad to the moon. It took more than the United States Congress to discourage him, and in 1844 he proved to the world that the telegraph is a success. The world then came to his side, and his fame spread abroad. Today his machines are clicking everywhere, sending telegraphic messages around the world.

Two young men in a small Ohio town had a little

Airplanes have changed greatly from the Wright brothers' plane shown in the lower picture.

bicycle shop, and in their spare time experimented on a flying machine. The world called them both lazy and crazy, but they kept on with their experiments until they had built a machine which would fly. Being patriotic Americans, they offered the United States first chance at their invention. The government wrote back, "We cannot consider your suggestion that we buy your inventions or that we send a commission to investigate them. We have neither time nor money to waste on a couple of Ohio cranks. We are not interested.

Though they were the subjects of jokes, ridicule and scorn, their faith was unshaken, and they went on to victory. Don't expect that the world will always extend a helping hand.

In the year 1359 a dried-up little clerk by the name of Geoffrey Chaucer was a guest of the English army, which was laying siege to a French town. He was not a soldier, but a poet, and because of his ability as a "scribbler of rhymes," the king pensioned him, and the officers of the army bestowed many favors upon him.

If an officer, a soldier, or a body of troops showed any cowardice, Chaucer would write a verse, or verses, making sport of their weakness. In a few hours the whole army was singing their failures. This worked magic, and the next time the individual soldier or company was given a dangerous task, they went at it fearlessly, for they would rather be shot than to be made fun of or laughed at.

Not many of us can stand to be laughed at. A good many people have faced guns, but couldn't face ridicule. It is not difficult to travel along with the crowd. When our friends pat us on the back and say that they believe in us, we can carry on all right; but let them turn their backs on us, and criticize and condemn, and we will become discouraged unless we have a real vision and a backbone.

George Westinghouse conceived the idea of stopping trains with an air brake, and went to one of the wealthy men of New York to interest him in the invention. The millionaire received his card, but sent back word that he didn't have any time to waste with fools who talked of stopping trains with wind.

Fortunately Westinghouse was a man who could stand rebuff. To be called a fool did not discourage him. He still believed in his invention, and today the trains of the world, and many large trucks, are using it.

New Jersey farmers rejected the first successful cast-iron plow invented in the United States. They declared that the cast iron would poison the land and stimulate the growth of noxious weeds.

There is no printed record of any one's encouraging Robert Fulton when he was experimenting with a steamboat which would do away with the old hand-propelled boats. Mobs followed him through the streets, calling him a fool, and his boat was named "Fulton's Folly." Those who loaned him money asked that their names be withheld, for they did not wish to be classed as fools also for supporting such a project. Those who gathered on the Hudson to see the trial trip of the boat said, "It will never go." But it worked, and those who had come to scoff remained to praise him.

At this time Napoleon was master of Europe, and had a heart-longing to conquer the world. But he must take England, which meant crossing the English Channel with his army. To do this he must have some sort of craft which would out-travel the British fleet. Robert

Fulton called on Napoleon and offered to sell him his invention. He could then cross the Channel with boats propelled by steam. It was a real opportunity for Napoleon, but he turned down the offer. Why? He feared that it might fail, and he would be the laughing stock of the world. He couldn't stand to be laughed at. Had he bought the steamboat invention, history might have been different.

When Christopher Columbus became convinced that our world was round and that he could reach the East by sailing west, he went to King John of Portugal and told the monarch of his ideas. The scheme looked good to King John and he could see that if it should work, it might make Portugal the greatest country in the world. But—suppose it should fail. His councilors showed him that he would be laughed at if he should give support to such a foolhardy enterprise. And as King John couldn't stand to be laughed at, he said, "No," to Columbus.

Columbus immediately went to Spain, and there, too, the wise men of the court said that he was crazy. But Queen Isabella saw light in the theories of Columbus, and she didn't care what the world thought. She supplied the funds for ships and supplies, declaring that she would sell her jewels, if necessary, to secure funds. As a result of her fearlessness and the ability of Columbus to face derision and scorn, America was discovered.

Galileo, the astronomer, spent twelve of the best years of his life in prison for teaching that the earth is only one of the several planets which constitute our solar system. But he believed it.

Bruno was burned at the stake in Rome in 1620 for teaching that there are other worlds than ours, and that instead of there being but one solar system, there are many such systems throughout infinite space. He had opinions of his own, and they were so dear to him that he was willing to die rather than to surrender them.

When the promoters of a railroad tried to get a right of way through the country, they met opposition on every hand. An eloquent clergyman in the United States declared that the inhabitants of the country would be driven mad by the sight of the locomotives rushing through the land, and many insane asylums would have to be built to care for them.

A school board in Ohio refused to let the promoters hold a meeting in the school house in their community. They felt the railroad would ruin the country, and that God had never intended that man should rush through space at the speed of fifteen miles an hour. Experts in Germany proved (?) to the public that travelers on trains going at fifteen miles an hour would suffer from nosebleed and that there would be danger of suffocation when going through tunnels.

The first steam fire engine was demonstrated in 1828 in London by Ericsson, but the municipal government was so prejudiced against it that they continued to use an old hand pump for thirty-two years. The world has been slow to accept new ideas.

The inventor of a weaving machine was caused to be strangled by the Council of Danzig in the sixteenth century. They feared his invention would throw men out of work.

In 1842 Adam Thompson constructed the first bathtub in North America. But bathtubs were not popular. Some localities put a heavy tax on every tub installed. Boston passed a bylaw prohibiting their use except when ordered by a physician. They agreed that they might be all right in summer, but in winter their use would result in sickness and death.

The editor of a Springfield paper received an invitation to ride in an automobile, when the machine was just coming on the market. He refused. "It is incompatible with the dignity of my position," he declared.

Chauncey Depew felt "nothing could come along to beat the horse." So he advised a nephew of his not to invest money in Ford stocks. That didn't stop Mr. Ford, however, and the people who did invest in his gas buggy in those early days soon became rich.

Public opinion has been opposed to anything, yes everything, which showed signs of improvement or betterment. Public opinion told Edison that no machine could be made to talk. It told McCormick that he was wasting his time in working on a reaper, for a machine could never tie a knot.

The *New York World* printed the following news item on its front page in 1868:

"A man about 43 years of age, giving the name of Joshua Coppersmith, has been arrested for attempting to extort funds from ignorant and superstitious people by exhibiting a device which he says will convey the human voice over metallic wires. He calls the instrument a 'telephone,' which is obviously intended to imitate the word telegraph and win the confidence of those who know of the success of the latter instrument. Well informed people know that it is impossible to transmit the human voice over wires as may be done with signals of the Morse code. The authorities who apprehended this criminal are to be congratulated, and it is hoped that his punishment will be prompt, and for a long prison duration."

When rayon first appeared on the market, silk manufacturers declared it to be "just a transient fad." When the tractor came, bankers refused to lend money on it, for they felt it was a "menace to farmers."

Right has usually been in the minority. The wrong way is usually crowded, and often leads downhill. It is easy going. One cannot be right and always travel with the crowds or have the applause of men. You may have to stand alone, while the world looks on with scorn. To do this, one must know he is right. But when we feel we are right, we should be willing to stand alone if necessary.

We cannot drift into goodness. We will have to face the wind, to battle with the tide.

Inventory Time

AS A BOY I worked in a general store, and I couldn't understand just why, once a year, we had to go to the trouble of measuring every yard of cloth, weighing every keg of nails, counting the cards of buttons, estimating the gallons of gasoline in the tank, reckoning the value of every tin of canned goods, weighing the sugar, beans, cornmeal, etc. I dreaded the task, for there were so many tiny articles to count and list, as well as numberless items of larger value. We handled everything in the hardware line from pins to barbed wire. We sold shoes, yard goods, groceries, in fact, most anything one might need.

It soon dawned upon my undeveloped brain that this was the only way the firm could tell, at the end of the year, whether they had made a gain as a result of their business transactions, or if, after all our labor, they were worse off financially than when the year began. Firms record either a loss or a gain at the close of the year.

So it is with individuals. We are either better or worse now than we were a year ago. Too many of us, after a certain time in life, feel that we are holding our own—not growing, but standing still. In reality, we are either growing or shriveling—progressing or backsliding.

It was Nicholas Murray Butler who said that the epitaph of most men might be written on their tombstones in these words, "Dead at Thirty—Buried at Sixty."

This is a brief biography of many a life. At thirty

A store could not operate if it did not take inventory sometimes.

growth stopped—no new ideas were acquired after that, no lessons learned, no effort for self or for others, no new friendships made, no seed sown after thirty, and no harvests gathered in. Just at the time in life when we have had experience enough to really begin to live, too many of us settle down complacently to do nothing the rest of our days.

It may be some trouble to take inventory, but we will be well repaid when we do it. As we look back over the year which has gone, we will find a story either of growth or retrogression. Are we better citizens than a year ago? Have we grown as a companion in the home— as father, mother, brother, sister, or friend? Have we built up our health, or have we formed habits which are tearing us down physically? How about the spiritual side of our nature? Are we as faithful in our devotions, in church attendance, in helping our fellow men, in giving of our means to support the church and its activities? If we haven't grown, we have slipped back. There has been no "just holding our own."

A father, whose young son was dear to his heart, had been keeping tab on the little fellow's growth by having him stand up against the door casing and marking his height every now and then. At each measuring, the happy little fellow had grown "just a bit." The mark was slowly creeping higher and higher. It was difficult to tell whether the father or the son was the more pleased at the growth the child was making. One day, when his height had been carefully recorded, and it was found he had grown a quarter of an inch since the last check-up, the proud little fellow looked up into his father's face and asked very earnestly, "Daddy, do you still grow?"

That question set the fond parent to thinking. All

through the day it kept coming back, pressing for an answer. After he went to bed, he thought of it still. He was getting a real thrill in watching the growth of his son, but had he quit growing?

It is a good question for us to ask ourselves. Are we still growing? Did we grow last year? Will we grow next year? The answer for the future lies with us. We shall either grow or shrivel. This inventory business may be a bit tedious to us, but it will do us all good.

Don't Be Too Hasty!

WE HAD at our house a little bantam rooster, just a mite of a fellow. He wasn't homely at all, and may have had some reasons for strutting about so proudly. Even though small in stature, he acted about as important as any chicken I have ever seen, regardless of size or pedigree. The first thing he did in the morning was to get up on some prominent place and crow and crow and crow, seeming to be anxious to have the world know about him, and fearful lest his importance should not be recognized.

His little mate, a brown bantam hen, was modest and shy. She was busy all the day, scratching and working, and occasionally slipped quietly away to the nest to lay an egg. Not once did I hear her cackle about her accomplishments, either. My wife and I talked about these two chickens, and came to the conclusion that the little hen was the better part of the team, and that she did a great deal more, and said a lot less, about it. We rather criticized the little rooster for his proud, arrogant manner, and for his crowing.

But a day or so later I told my wife that I thought we had been a little hasty in forming our conclusions, for, after all, I discovered that this little rooster had some very fine traits. One, in particular, I would like to mention. And when I sized the little fellow up, after knowing him better, I felt that I really owed him an apology. I was spading garden close to the bantam home the next day after we had classed the little rooster as a proud egotist who did a great deal of crowing about nothing. I found a large number of fine fat worms as I turned over the soil, and, knowing the weakness of chickens, I tossed these over the fence.

Every time a worm went over the fence, that little rooster called his mate. He would chatter away, saying something which I imagine meant for her to come in a hurry. And he would pick the worm up in his bill and toss it toward her so she could see it. I threw a good many worms over the fence, but not one did that little fellow eat. He gave every one of them to the little hen. She ate them without any hesitation. I tried the same with corn and other feed. Each time he made that same loving sound, and then stood and watched Biddy eat the food. I suppose that he did eat sometimes, for he looked well fed. But he surely stood by and saw that she got her share first. He was unselfishness personified.

Perhaps you will think that we are running short of material when we have to write about bantam chickens, but I got a lesson from this experience. I had been a little too quick in forming my opinion. I was ready to criticize the little bantam at the first weakness I noticed. I was ready to put him in the "no good" class. But I found, on watching him and getting better acquainted, that he really had some wonderful qualities.

As we stand aside and watch our fellow men we are apt to jump at conclusions. One fault or shortcoming is noticed, and we form opinions. We criticize, find fault, and condemn. We tell others about the faults and failings of our brother; we magnify them. But if we would just withhold our criticisms, and try to get a little better acquainted—if we would just wait a while and look beneath the surface—we might find many qualities which offset the little weaknesses we have noticed.

And how true it is that we see what we look for. If we habitually look for the bad in our fellow men, we are apt to find some unlovely things, for none are perfect; yet, if we look for the good in our loved ones, our neighbors, our friends, we will be sure to find it, for be a man ever so bad there is surely some good in him.

Have you had feelings in your heart against some particular race or nation? Have you been prejudiced against certain religious organizations? Have you criticized and condemned men and women before you really knew them? Don't be too hasty in forming opinions.

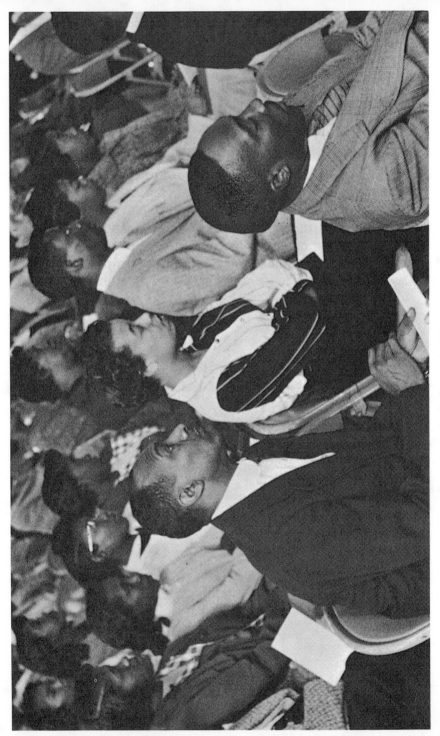

Almost everybody listened with great attention.

Sermons We See

A SUCCESSFUL evangelist had preached a powerful sermon, and there was a feeling of awe and solemnity in the great auditorium. He closed his discourse with an earnest appeal that all who were not Christians might yield their lives to Christ.

More than a score answered his appeal and went forward for prayer. Among them was a woman in middle life, well dressed, and having every mark of refinement and culture.

She asked the evangelist if she might say a few words, and permission was granted her to speak. A hush fell over the large audience as she began.

"I would like to tell you," she said, "just why I have come forward tonight—just why I want to be a Christian. It is not because of the eloquent words spoken by the preacher. I am giving my life to God because of the influence of a dear little woman who is in the audience tonight. Her form is bent by the hard work of many years. Her hands are red and horny from constant daily toil. She is just an unknown, obscure, but faithful washwoman. For many years she has been a servant in my home. Never once in these many years has this faithful soul ever complained or been impatient. Her way has been hard, and she has had more than her share of trials and troubles. But she has always manifested the same sweet Christian spirit. Not one unkind word has she uttered in my presence, even when my harshness might have provoked and irritated her. Not a cloud ever crossed her countenance in my presence. Her life has been adorned with little acts of unselfishness and love. Day by day her thoughts have been of others.

"A short time ago my little girl was snatched from me, and I was broken-hearted and without hope. This little woman brought joy and gladness into my barren, empty life. She read to me from the Bible about life beyond the grave, and gave to me my first ray of hope. I began to long for that something which made her life so beautiful. It was her sweet Christian influence which led me to Christ."

The minister called the embarrassed little woman down to the front and then introduced this humble soul as the real preacher of the evening. He admonished his congregation to go from the meeting to do likewise—to preach by their daily lives; for as the poet has said, people "would rather see a sermon, than hear one any day."

Friendly Counsel--No Fees

A FEW years ago there appeared in a popular monthly magazine this unusual advertisement:

> "Believing that some men and women are burdened and anxious, and need help in meeting perplexing personal problems, a physician, retired from general practice, offers not medical advice, but friendly counsel. No fees. By appointment only. —Box 779."

It was such a simple advertisement, and yet so sincere, that many troubled souls were led to answer it. And today Dr. Addison Baird, the retired physician who wrote that notice, has told us that hundreds of men and women have come to him for help, counsel, and guidance. Among these troubled souls were rich and poor, young and old. They talked to him about their hopes and fears, their joys and sorrows, sins, temptations, and failures. His office was in New York City, and in that great, throbbing, buzzing beehive of humanity, where selfishness is so evident, there are many in need of a friend. To these many sorely tried and tempted souls, the doctor has brought light and hope and joy.

Troubles are not confined to the New York area. We all have our ups and downs. No one of us passes through life without our trials and disappointments. You have yours and I have mine. Have you ever wished there was some real true friend near by to whom you could go for sympathy, counsel, and help?

There may not be a Doctor Baird in your community, but there is One to whom we all may go with the smallest and most trivial of our problems. "There is a friend that sticketh closer than a brother" (Proverbs 18:24), who is interested in all our joys and sorrows. Has He not told us that "the very hairs of your head are all numbered" (Luke 12:7), and that He marks the sparrow's fall? (Matthew 10:29-31.) And has He not invited us, "Come unto Me, all ye that labor and are heavy laden, and I will give you rest"? (Matthew 11:28.)

Jesus is the Friend of all, rich and poor, high and low, white, brown, red, yellow, or black. He has traveled life's road and knows all the temptations to which we are subject.

No appointment is necessary. There are no fees. All may come to Him by day or night, "and His ears are open unto their prayers." 1 Peter 3:12. In these hectic, trying times it is well to know such a friend.

Is Prejudice Robbing You?

WILLIAM, the water does not taste right," said a good housewife to her husband one morning when he had just brought a bucket of fresh water from the spring. "There must be something wrong," she continued. "Go down into the cellar, and see if there is anything in the spring."

This was almost a half century ago, before the public waterworks had come to their town. Every one depended upon his own well or water supply of some kind. Every one caught rainwater and kept it in the old-fashioned rainbarrel or cistern, but for drinking water there had to be other sources.

This family depended upon a spring of fine, cold, clear, sparkling water that gushed freely from the sandy bed beneath their cellar floor. It had been carefully inclosed with slabs of stone and a wooden door placed over the top to keep the water from becoming contaminated. There was an overflow pipe that led to a mossy wooden tub near the kitchen door, and from the tub the water overflowed, and ran lazily down to the mill pond near the barn.

Heeding his wife's bidding, William hastened to the cellar to investigate. It was only an illusion, he felt sure, but he would go to satisfy her. Raising the wooden cover, he saw a white object floating on the surface of the clear, sparkling spring. With a net he dipped it up, and found it to be a rat that in some way had gotten into the spring, and from all appearances had been a long time dead, so long that it was all puffed up and the hair had entirely

217

disappeared. Without any ceremony, the rodent was hurriedly buried in the barnyard.

Forty-five years have come and gone since then. The city waterworks have come, and it is no longer necessary for William and his wife to use the water of the spring. But it is still there in the basement flowing copiously and gurgling out into the moss-covered tub by the kitchen door, and on into the mill pond.

On hot summer days people come from far and near with their pails and jugs, and carry away the cool, refreshing water from the spring. "That is wonderful water, William," they say. "You can't find water like that often. Many thanks, William."

"Just help yourself," says William. "Drink all you like, and take all you want."

But never a drop will William drink. If he were choking, he would not touch it, for he still sees the rat of forty-five years ago. The water is pure and fresh, but there is prejudice in William's heart, and prejudice doesn't allow a man to reason, to be sensible. And William is the loser. Somebody has well said:

"Prejudice never quite dies. Hit it in the head with an ax, strangle it, drown it, hang it, burn it, poison it, do what you will with it, and when it ought to be properly dead by all rules of the game, it bobs up again to haunt one. Prejudice never forgets and never forgives. Argument does not move it or proof convince; and there it is tattooed into the brain forever."

One evening a man stood in front of a town hall where they were discussing better schools. Some one who happened to be passing inquired what the meeting was about. "I don't know," the man replied; "all I do know is that, whatever it is, I'm agin it."

Webster says prejudice is "opinion adverse to anything without just grounds or before sufficient knowledge
of facts is obtained." It is insidious, hateful, and con-
demning without a trial. Doors of nations have been
closed to progress by this monster called prejudice.
Communities have been held back, robbed by the
dwarfed minds of those who refused to learn new truths.
Individuals have closed the door to untold blessings because they shut their minds against new ideas, new light.

When I was a boy, I refused to eat lettuce. Mother
begged me just to try it once, hoping that I might learn
to like it. "No, I don't like it," I argued. "I don't want
any of that grass for mine."

I had never tasted it, and knew nothing about the
vitamins it contained, the very things my system was
calling for. But poor, ignorant, foolish creature, I decided without knowledge. I was the loser, of course.

When the bathtub was first introduced, people could
not be induced to use it. Prejudiced they were, of course,
and they were not going to kill themselves by taking a
bath in winter. They were too wise for that.

In civil law an individual who is suspected of crime
is always allowed a trial before he is sentenced. A jury
of twelve men is usually chosen, men who have not been
prejudiced by information already received. The facts
are heard, the alleged criminal is given a chance to de-
fend himself, and then sentence is passed or the accused
is acquitted.

If you and I were only as fair in making our conclusions, we would be far better off. We are not nearly so
fair in our dealings with one another—yes, and with ourselves. We meet an individual for the first time, look him
over, and if he doesn't dress just as we think he should or

talk to suit us, if he doesn't just appeal to our tastes and
fancies, we decide we won't like him, and we rather os-
tracize him. It is a cruel thing to do, but we are the ones
who suffer.

For a long time I was prejudiced against night air,
and tried to exclude it from my sleeping room. A little
draft of fresh air at night would start me on the road to
the undertaker, I felt sure. I wonder how I could have
been so ignorant. Night air is no different from day air;
and now I can't sleep without it, because I know it is in-
vigorating and health-giving. But I lost a great deal
through prejudice.

The Chinese for years have shut out the civilization
of the West, preferring to ride in wheelbarrows, to dig
the soil with the hoe and the old wooden plow, and to
travel in the paths of their ancestors. They have been
prejudiced against western civilization. Who has been
the loser?

When Noah talked of a flood, people said, "It has
never rained here, and it never will. There can be no
flood." When Luther affirmed that the church had been
mistaken in some of her teachings and that men could
be justified by simple faith in God, they were ready to
kill him. Columbus had a hard time to find anyone open-
minded enough even to consider his theory that the earth
was round. "It is flat," men affirmed, and that settled it.
The Wright brothers were declared crazy by some when
they first talked of flying. What we don't understand we
oppose.

In every age God has had new truth to impart to His
children, a message for that particular time. The great
majority have usually shut their eyes, their ears, and
their minds and hearts to this message, it is true, but

there always have been some who were honest, broad-minded, and unprejudiced. The great majority were prejudiced in Noah's time. But who were the losers?

I have allowed prejudice to warp my judgment, to narrow my vision, and to rob me of many blessings. I have lost much by binding, blinding prejudice, and I have pretty well learned my lesson. Let me hear the facts before I decide. It may hurt me to change my ways of thinking and doing, but it pays in the end, for it always brings blessing.

You have your ideas, and you are entitled to them. Some of them may be right, and it is possible some of them may be wrong. Hold to them until you are satisfied they are wrong, and then be man or woman enough to admit your wrong and to change your ways. But don't condemn until you have listened to the evidence and weighed it carefully.

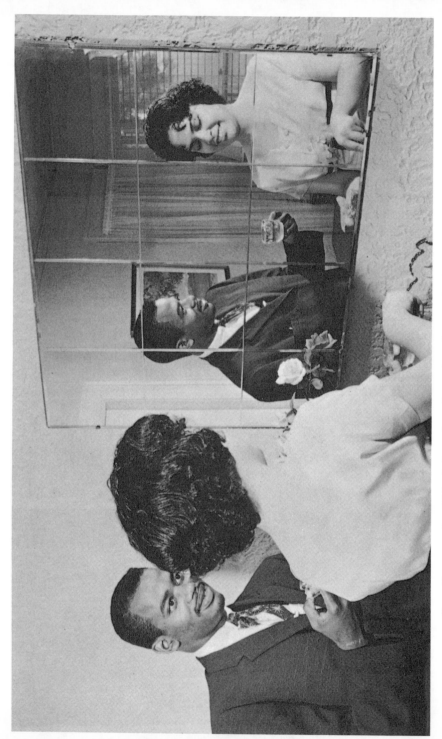

Sometimes we should look into the mirror that shows what kind of persons we are.

Don't Break Your Looking Glass

THE STORY is told of a beautiful Englishwoman who lived about two centuries ago—Lady Montague. Clever and attractive in her youth, she came to the time in life when her mirror told of wrinkles, gray hairs, and vanishing charms. In her desperation she had all her mirrors destroyed, and as the story goes, from that day until her death, she refused to look into a looking glass again. She couldn't face the facts; she didn't want to know her true condition. Her beauty was fading, youth was giving place to old age, and she didn't like to have her mirror tell her the truth. A silly and childish thing to do, of course, but how many of us are big enough to face the facts, to be told the truth about ourselves?

From the windows of his castle a European monarch looked out daily over the burying ground of his ancestors. Daily he was reminded of the frailty of man, and knew full well that he too must someday go the "way of all the earth." Someday he must yield the scepter to another; someday some one else would ascend his throne. These thoughts troubled him. So he ordered another castle built, with a different outlook. He didn't want to be reminded daily that he too must "pass through the portals of death." It wasn't pleasant for him to think that his reign of authority, luxury, and ease must someday end.

Your mirror and mine tell us that the years have brought changes in our faces and forms. But there is no use destroying the friendly looking glass. We should face the facts. There are mirrors, too, which tell us of

223

conditions on the side—in our minds and in our hearts.

After all, it does not make so much difference about this body of ours, but we should be deeply concerned about the life. Christ's life and God's law have been given us as mirrors, that we may check up on our inner selves—that we may know just what progress we are making.

We often check up on our looks—the outer man—but how often do we take inventory of the inner man? We consult the mirror a good many times a day to see to our outward appearance, but how often do we take a glance at the looking glass which pictures our real self? And how many of us are willing to be told of our faults and failings?

We are like the young man who was driving through the countryside with an old-fashioned minister of the gospel. The young man was just old enough to feel that he knew more than any one else in the world, and delighted in arguing about the Scriptures. The wise old preacher listened without much comment, as the modern young fellow expressed his views.

Finally, the parson had a chance to get in a word, "So you object to the Ten Commandments, do you?"

"N-no," stammered the young man, "not their purpose and object—but—well, a fellow hates to have a 'shall' and 'shan't' flung in his face every minute! They sound so contrary!"

Trying to hide a smile, the old minister said not a word, but clucked to his horse and drove on quietly. They hadn't gone far when the boy grabbed his arm and exclaimed, "You have taken the wrong road. Didn't you see that signboard at the fork in the road? It said that the other road is the way to Taunton."

"Is that right?" said the old gentleman carelessly. "Maybe it is a better road, but I do hate to be told to go this way or that by an arbitrary old signpost."

He didn't need to say any more, for the young man got the lesson. They turned about and were soon following the road pointed out by the signboard.

The Bible has been given us as a guide on life's way. It tells us "this is the way, walk ye in it." Isaiah 30:21. It reproves of sin, points out our defects. And it often reveals our real selves so plainly that it bothers the conscience.

Outwardly, we are growing older with the years. We are getting more wrinkles and gray hairs, stooped shoulders, and slackened gait. But inwardly we should be growing in grace—becoming better, more like our Pattern, as the days fly by. So while the mirrors which hang on our walls may have a discouraging story to tell us, the mirror of God's word should tell us a message of comfort and hope—tell us we are adding virtue to virtue.

Break the mirror if you will, but the wrinkles increase just the same. Discard the Bible; do away with the Ten Commandments in your life, and the sin will still be there. Tear down the signboard at the crossroads if you feel that way, but the destination at the end of the way is always the same.

"The wages of sin is death," and we might just as well face the facts. (Romans 6:23.) The Ten Commandments have been given us as a guide and compass, and Christ's life as a pattern. Are we keeping all the commandments? Are we patterning our life after His? Destroy the looking glass if you will, but keep every precept of His law. Discard the plate-glass mirror if you feel so inclined, but keep ever before you the mirror of

Christ's life which will reveal the true condition of the inner man. Be big enough to face the facts, to look your faults squarely in the face. And be honest with yourself, and "add to your faith virtue; and to virtue knowledge; and to knowledge temperance; and to temperance patience; and to patience godliness; and to godliness brotherly kindness; and to brotherly kindness charity." 2 Peter 1:5-7.

God Keeps His Word

SOME months ago I was in the city of Chicago, on my way West. And because of Chicago's reputation, one is naturally inclined to be a little suspicious of strangers. I hurried into the Union Station late at night to buy a railroad ticket. Every man and woman in the corridors and waiting rooms was a stranger to me. At the ticket window I met a man who was a stranger to me also. I had never seen him before, and have not seen him since. I asked about trains and the fare, and he asked me for more than $100 for a ticket to California and back to Chicago.

I took from my pocket some good paper money and passed it through the wicket to this stranger, who, in return, gave me only a narrow strip of green paper, which pomised me a first-class passage to California and back. Did I doubt him? No, I passed over the money and took that piece of green paper in return without the least hesitation. I picked up my bag and started for the train, but was stopped near the gate, where the conductor, another stranger, seated at a high desk, asked for this precious ticket, and I had to surrender it to him. He folded it up carefully, and put it in an envelope and slipped it into his pocket. He handed me a small check, and promised that my ticket would be returned before I left the train at San Francisco. Did I worry about it? Not a bit.

I checked a piece of baggage on that train, too. It had taken me some time to gather together the valuables in that hand baggage, but I surrendered it to a strange man in the big city of Chicago, and he gave me a small

"I had no idea who was to drive that great engine while I slept that night. But I went to sleep without a care."

piece of cardboard about three by two inches, with some figures printed on it. That was my security. Did I lose my baggage? No. I trusted these railway employees, and they cared for my belongings. That train was manned by a crew who were strangers to me also. I had no idea who was to drive that great engine while I slept that night. But I went to sleep without a care. The old train rambled on through the darkness, over bridges, past switches, around curves, and I slept peacefully on, trusting my life to those strangers. Hadn't they promised me on that green ticket that they would carry me safely to my destination? Yes, they had promised, and I had faith to believe they would.

The Lord has made hundreds, yes, thousands of promises in His word. They have been recorded for us. Do we believe them? We trust frail, erring man, but do we have faith in God?

If you should feel a severe pain in your lower right side, you probably would consult a physician, who might tell you you need an operation immediately for appendicitis. You might be far from home, among total strangers. But you would climb onto an operating table and place your life in the hands of a strange surgeon and strange nurses. Mere man is not always dependable, but God "is not slack concerning His promise." 2 Peter 3:9. If we have faith in our fellow men, why can we not trust our heavenly Father?

Faith in God is one of the conditions of answered prayer. Without faith it is impossible to believe Him. And believing in Him as our Father, we will naturally pray, "Thy will be done," trusting that He will answer our prayers in the way that will be best for us.

George Muller was one time telling a friend how his

faith had increased in twenty-five years. The friend was
curious to know the secret, and inquired of Mr. Muller.
Raising aloft a copy of a wellworn Bible, he said,
"Friend, I have read the Book through 100 times.   I
know the Book, and I know the God of the Book."

Have you ever tried this prescription? In the Scriptures we are told, "Faith cometh by hearing, and hearing by the word of God." Romans 10:17. Because the
Bible is not read, is neglected, our generation stands
out as an unbelieving, faithless one.

The late Dr. David Paulson was on good terms with
the Master, and talked to Him often. He went to God
with simple requests, and He answered his prayers.
When he and his wife went out to a suburb of Chicago
to start the sanitarium, they were without funds. As
they were clearing off the weeds and underbrush from
the property which they had secured, they knelt down
on the hillside and told the Lord they needed $100 with
which to begin their work.   The second day after this a
man walked into the office of Dr. Paulson's brother in
Chicago, and asked if the doctor needed any money in
his work. When told that he did, he left $100 with Mr.
Paulson, and asked him to give it to the doctor. Did he
just happen to think about giving this money? Did it
just happen that he gave one hundred dollars instead of
seventy-five or eighty?

At one time the coal bin was empty at the Rescue
Home for Girls. The matron told her trouble to Dr.
Paulson, and he asked her if she had prayed about it.

"What!" she asked, rather surprised, "would you
pray for coal?"

"Why not?" replied the doctor. "Get your workers
together, and we will tell the Lord our needs."

The little family of workers came together in the chapel. Dr. Paulson knelt with them, and they told the Lord about the coal bin being empty, and asked Him to see that it was filled. That same week a letter came to the doctor, addressed in a trembling hand. It was from an elderly woman in southern Illinois. She felt impressed that the doctor needed money, and so sent him a check for $200. He had never seen this woman, but she had read of his work, and the Lord impressed her heart to send this check in answer to prayer. This was just the amount needed to buy a carload of coal.

These incidents did not happen only in Daniel's time, nor in the time of George Muller, but in our time—the twentieth century. God has not changed with the passing of the years. But we have changed, and have changed much. Nothing is wrong on the broadcasting end of the heavenly radio, but on the receiving end there are weaknesses.

At one time Dr. Paulson took fifteen nurses to Chicago to do community nursing. They asked the Lord to send them work for these fifteen young people, and within thirty-six hours the telephone rang just fifteen times, asking for nurses of that very kind.

Dr. Paulson needed a stenographer, and asked God to send him one. A ragged-looking man walked into his office a few days later and asked to see the doctor. On being asked what he wanted, he said he was looking for work. "What can you do?" asked the doctor. "I am a stenographer, sir," he answered.

"Well," said Dr. Paulson, "I have been praying for a stenographer."

"And I have been praying for work," said the stranger.

"I think we should get down on our knees," said the doctor, "and thank the Lord that we met—that He answered our prayers."

And they knelt together and thanked the Lord for answered prayer. Do we thank Him for His blessings, and for answering our prayers? That stenographer proved to be a good one, and helped around the sanitarium for many months. Would God do as much for you and me? Why wouldn't He?

Then What?

"IF I SHOULD ever be fortunate enough to own this beautiful estate, I would be very happy," said a young man to his friend, as they walked over the green fields and wooded slopes of a valuable rural property.

In a beautiful spot on the estate, surrounded by nature at its best, sat the medieval castle. The place was very appealing in its sylvan loveliness.

"Yes," said the young man, "if I had a deed to this place, I'd be very happy."

Looking the youth straight in the eye, his companion earnestly asked, "What then?"

After a brief pause the aspiring young gentleman replied, "Then I would pull down that old castle and build a comfortable modern home. Here I would invite my friends, and we would enjoy together the luxuries of life."

"Then what?"

"Then I'd get blooded horses, high-powered cars, servants, and fine clothes. I'd travel around the world. When at home, I'd invite my friends in, and we would dine, dance, drink fine wines, smoke, and live in luxury."

"What then?"

"I suppose I would grow old like other people, and in my old age live a more quiet life. I would settle down then."

"And what next?"

"Well, I imagine that I'd have to leave this home, its luxuries, and my friends. I'd die as others have died, and be buried in an expensive mausoleum."

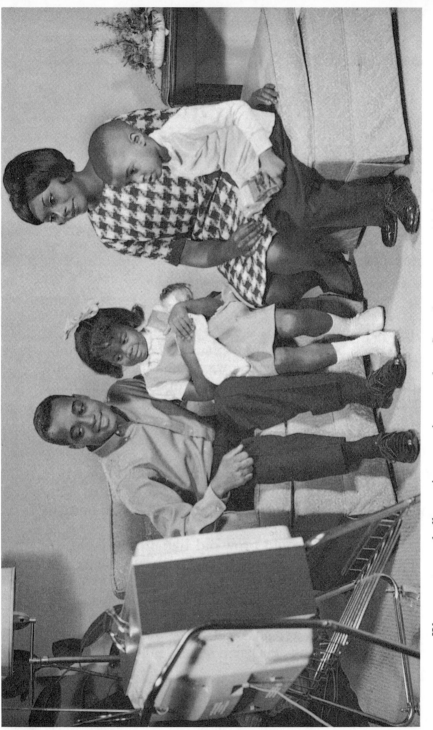

We cannot spend all our time amusing ourselves. Someday we must think about the future.

"And then?"

"Then—then—." He paused as if pondering. "Oh, forget about your 'thens'! I haven't any longer to talk about such things. I must be going."

So the two friends parted.

But the young fellow could not get away from that question, "What then?" Years later, when he met his questioning friend, he had answered that question. It did not worry him now. "God bless you, old friend," he said, "You were the means of entirely changing the course of my life."

"How?" inquired the friend.

"By a question you asked me some years ago—'What then?'"

It is a question we might each ask ourselves.

PHOTO AND ART CREDITS

OTHER REPRINTS NOW AVAILABLE

MAY BE ORDERED FROM YOUR LOCAL BOOK STORE

STORIES WORTH REREADING
73 stories originally compiled in 1913 to provide children and youth with stories that inspire, instruct, and entertain. Gathered from nearly 20 different publishers including Fleming H. Revell, D. L. Moody, Mennonite, Etc. A treasure house for pastors, teachers, and others who tell childrens stories.320 pages, 5-1/2 x 8-1/2, $7.95 1-881545-01-6

SABBATH READINGS for the HOME CIRCLE
Nearly 60 stories and 30 poems gathered during the 1870's. Originally compiled to provide families with suitable sabbath reading. Stories gathered from church papers; Methodist, Lutheran, Presbyterian, etc. Well illustrated. 400 pages, 5-1/2 x 8-1/2, $7.95 1-881545-02-4

CHOICE STORIES for CHILDREN
Over 40 stories gathered from several sources to provide children with the best character building literature. Excellent reading for the family that cares. Well illustrated. 136 pages, 6 x 8-1/4, Four color cover, $6.95 1-878726-08-0

THE KING'S DAUGHTER And Other Stories For Girls
Over 40 stories and 100 illustrations from the turn of the century. Every story contains an important lesson. Excellent reading for the family circle and of special interest for girls. 224 pages, 4-1/2 x 7, Four color cover, $4.95 ISBN 1-878726-04-8

TIGER AND TOM And Other Stories For Boys
Nearly 40 stories and 100 illustrations compiled as a companion to The King's Daughter. Excellent for boys. These books are character building at its best. They are a treasure to have. 224 pages,4-1/2 x 7, Four color cover, $4.95 ISBN 1-878726-06-4

LITTLE JOURNEYS INTO STORYLAND
Over 40 well illustrated stories that live and lift. Several short biographical sketches of prominent Blacks.235 pages,5-1/2x8-1/2,Four color cover,$6.95 ISBN 1-881545-06-7

WITHIN THE PALACE GATES
Author Anna Siviter
"Anna Siviter, by weaving the rich tapestry of the ancient Persian court as a backdrop for the story of Artaxerxes's noble cupbearer, allows us to grasp the deep significance of Nehemiah's devotion to God, to Jerusalem and to his people...." June Strong Originally published in 1901.320 pages, 5-1/2x8-1/2, Four color cover, $7.95 ISBN 1-881545-11-3

CHRIST OUR SAVIOUR (Gift Edition)

Author. E. G. White

First published in 1896 for the sake of children and youth. Written especially that children might know Jesus as a personal friend and saviour. Well illustrated.184 pages, 6 x 8-1/4, Four color cover, $5.95 ISBN 1-878726-07-2

BEST STORIES FROM THE BEST BOOK (Gift Edition)

Author: J. E. White

The best in Bible stories and lessons for the family. "These things.....were written for our admoniation" Cor.10:11.This book is prefaced with an easy reader section for young children with many four color illustrations. 200 pages, 6 x 8-1/4 Four color cover, $6.95 ISBN 1-878726-03-x (Also in German Edition)

CHILD'S POEMS

Nearly 40 poetic stories complied in 1878 as a companion to Sabbath Readings and the Golden Grain Series. The same instructive values are taught. 128 pages, 4-1/4 x 6 $3.95 ISBN 1-878726-19-6

CHRIST'S OBJECT LESSONS

Author: E. G. White

Author uncovers new and deeper levels of meaning in more than 25 parables and metaphors. Eye-opening concepts and the new resevoirs of inspiration in every chapter.

432 pages, 5-1/2 x 8-1/2, Four color cover, $8.50 ISBN 1-878726-16-1.

EDUCATION

Author: E. G. White

It is rare, indeed, for a book devoted to the subject of education to be read so widely or to endure so well the tests of changing times as has the book Education.

You will find every chapter rich with biblical principles and insights. **Raymond Moore** quotes on back cover: "I regard the book, "*Education*', as the greatest spirtual book on the subject this side of the Bible. I have experimented with it's ideas and find them faultless". 324 pages, 5-1/2 x 8-1/2, Four color cover, $7.95, ISBN 1-878726-17-X